Issue 12 Summer 2018

Science fiction magazine from Scotland

ISSN 2059-2590
ISBN 978-1-9997002-7-0

Shoreline of Infinity is available in digital or print editions.
Submissions of fiction, art, reviews, poetry, non-fiction are welcomed:
visit the website to find out how to submit.

www.shorelineofinfinity.com

Publisher
Shoreline of Infinity Publications / The New Curiosity Shop
Edinburgh
Scotland

310518

Cover: Siobhan McDonald

Contents

Editorial Team

Co-founder, Editor & Editor-in-Chief:

Noel Chidwick

Co-founder, Art Director:

Mark Toner

Deputy Editor & Poetry Editor:

Russell Jones

Reviews Editor:

Iain Maloney

Assistant Editor & First Reader:

Monica Burns

Copy editors:

Iain Maloney, Russell Jones, Monica
Burns, Pippa Goldschmidt

Extra thanks to:

Jack Deighton, M Luke McDonell,
Katy Lennon, and many others.

First Contact

www.shorelineofinfinity.com

contact@shorelineofInfinity.com

Twitter: @shoreinf

and on Facebook

Pull Up a Log

Iain Maloney

Iain bows out gracefully as our Reviews Editor.
Many thanks for all yout hard work and great cheer.
–Ed. and the rest of the Shoreline team of weird characters

In issue 8½, I wrote about Scottish dystopias, looked into the rising tide of pessimism that was sweeping the nation's artists and readers. We live in interesting times and the outlook for many is bleak, and our science fiction – as science fiction always has – reflects this. Climate change. Populism. Dictators with nuclear weapons. Terrorism. Disease and mass extinctions. Cheery stuff.

The flipside of all this, the positive to keep in mind, is that it means our science fiction is in rude health. It's booming. In my role as reviews editor for the last ten issues I've been overwhelmed by choice. Emails from publicists, recommendations from friends, tweets from readers, there's just so much damn good science fiction out there we need an Asimovian timescale to read it all. And the diversity of it all. Science fiction is no longer the preserve of the spherically-challenged white man in an "I Believe" t-shirt: women, BAME writers, LGBTI authors, SF in translation. It's all over the book shops and all over our screens. Amazon, Netflix et al are tripping over themselves to adapt our classics. Maybe one day they'll get round to giving us the John Wyndham adaptations we deserve. *The Kraken Wakes? Please?*

It has never been so exciting to be a science fiction fan. For me, *Shoreline of Infinity* has played a big part in the excitement. When issue one came out in late 2015, the words 'Scottish science fiction magazine' caught my eye on Twitter. I bought the first issue, became a fan. I offered a review for issue two and by issue three I was in charge of the reviews. *Shoreline* is like any SF utopia – well run, friendly, always innovating and packed full of weird characters. It has been my honour to be one weird character among many but now I must take a step back. Samantha Dolan will be taking over from issue 13 and you'll be in safe hands. I'll continue to review for *Shoreline* but mainly I'm going to become a fan again. Too many stories, too little time. I need to read. I need to write. There's an infinity of stories out there and what is the point of a shoreline if not as somewhere to dive in from?

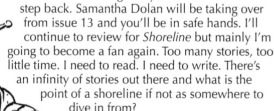

Follow Iain on twitter:
@iainmaloney

Do Not Pass GO

Helen Jackson

Art: Jackie Duckworth Art

"**I**t's fun for all the family," said the man from the bank. Joanna McGowan, adjustment marketer (Toys and Games), kept herself from sighing. A couple of minor mistakes and here she was, stuck with a pinstriped banker and a board game. She needed to get this one right. Another round of redundancies was rumoured, she was behind on the rent, and the jobs market for historians was bleak.

"When did you wish to market this concept?" she asked, following her script carefully. A recording of the briefing meeting would be timelocked, along with the contract.

"Our researchers favour the early years of the twentieth century."

Joanna nodded and looked down at the square board, her face neutral. The idea certainly wouldn't fly in Austerity Britain.

"Could you talk me through the gameplay?" she asked.

Charlie Compton began to detail an interminably long game where players invested in property and attempted to bankrupt each other, for fun. His blond fringe flapped as he gestured enthusiastically. His too-spicy aftershave filled the office. Joanna's mind wandered. She fiddled with the ends of her tangerine scarf, re-aligned the papers in front of her and watched clouds scud by outside. She had no interest in finance – which probably explained the size of her overdraft.

Eventually Compton stopped.

"What did you say the game was called?" Joanna asked.

"We're calling it 'Property is Best!'."

"Uh-huh," Joanna said, writing it down.

"And we don't wish to market it under the bank's name," Compton said. "Find someone appropriate to 'invent' the game and gift them the idea."

Even Joanna knew that made no financial sense.

"You won't earn a bonus with that business plan," she joked. Bankers' bonuses were all over the news, again.

Compton leaned forward. "I work hard for my bonus," he said, his voice rising. "I deserve it. I don't care what the left-wing media says." He slammed the palm of his right hand onto the desk. Joanna raised her eyebrows at the over-reaction. Compton took a deep breath and took his hand back, placing it gently in his lap. He spoke in a more measured tone.

"If everyone had grown up playing 'Property is Best!' they'd appreciate the capitalist system. There'd be less banker-bashing and more understanding of the valuable, difficult job we do."

Joanna made another "uh-huh" noise, worried about where the conversation was heading. Her license only covered marketing. If fat cat Compton intended to use his game as an ideological tool, then the project should be handed over to Political.

She considered consulting Head Office, upstream in the twenty-third century, but swiftly decided against. It would do her precarious employment situation no good at all if Compton spent his money in another department. He'd come to Toys and Games, and he'd stay in Toys and Games. She picked up the department's standard list of Key Performance Indicators and passed the page over to Compton.

"Is there a particular KPI you'd like us to focus on?" Joanna asked.

"Well, it's about reaching the masses. We'd like to see more positive headlines and—"

"Headlines and reach," said Joanna, cutting him off fast. No more politics! "Let's highlight visibility, measured through press cuttings, and units sold as your priorities. Our fee for the adjustment will be tied to these two measures. You won't remember this meeting, but when you receive our bill you can be confident the desired outcome has been achieved."

Joanna brought the meeting to a close as quickly as possible and saw Compton out of the building. She was sure she could get away with treating this as a routine marketing project as long as no further mention of childhood indoctrination was on the record.

"Ouch," Joanna said, yanking her head forward. The hairdresser sighed, gripped a hairpin in his mouth, and used both hands to move Joanna's head back into position. He carried on pulling, curling and pinning, ignoring her complaints.

Two hours later, scalp stinging, Joanna couldn't face getting straight into costume. She'd identified America in 1903 as the optimum target market for Compton's game, which meant undergarments almost as complicated as her hairdo. She popped across the road for a coffee instead.

Buying the bucket-sized beverage and tipping the barista left her purse empty. She balanced her cup precariously while she got money from an ATM and cursed as scalding latte ran up her wrist. The skin reddened and an ugly blister formed. She'd have to put a plaster on it; fortunately her long-sleeved costume would hide the anachronism.

Back in her office she polished off the coffee, suited up, and checked her notes. One Elizabeth Magie was her chosen contemporary. Magie had sold several games, without making her fortune. Joanna was certain she could interest the woman in another. She even had a plan which would allow her to bring up "Property is Best!" casually, thanks to a list of lecture attendees she'd found in a microfiched copy of the Brentwood Sentinel. She smiled to herself, pleased with her research.

"My dearest Joanna," said a drawling voice behind her, "I adore what you've done to your hair. The Gibson Girl look is very becoming."

Regency George stood in the doorway, in a navy frock coat, two waistcoats – of royal blue and canary yellow – and a pair of long trousers. Joanna hadn't seen her friend wearing trousers rather than breeches before. George had been born in the 1980s, but adopted the fashions of his chosen period with enthusiasm. He rarely wore post-1820 attire.

"Thanks, George. The curls took forever," Joanna said, carefully adding a wide-brimmed straw hat trimmed with peach silk roses. "You're looking rather... late."

"Certainly I am, m'dear. This charming get-up is 1833." He gestured down at himself ruefully. "I do miss the silk stockings."

"What brings you to Toys and Games?" George worked in Culture, specialising in Regency literature.

"Backgammon. I'm to introduce the demmy game to Thackeray in the hope he'll mention it in *Vanity Fair*. My client operates an online gaming table and wishes to 'increase backgammon's cultural presence'."

Joanna laughed. "Can you see Becky Sharpe playing backgammon? It's hardly her game! Those Pick-Up Sticks sessions demonstrate her steady nerves so well."

"Just you wait, m'dear," George said, heading on his way. "Just you wait."

Joanna placed herself at the back of the Friends' meetinghouse. She was in Brentwood, Maryland, February 1903. Daylight flooded in through large windows. Simple timber benches ran around three sides of the space, dark wood stark against white walls. Upright chairs had been set out for the lecture.

Elizabeth Magie sat in the front row, showing every sign of enthusiasm for the lecture's subject matter. Joanna could barely stay awake. Instead, she double-checked her outfit. The other women had considerably less elaborate hair, and plain bonnets rather than hats. *Quakers; I should have known.* Still, her ankle-length skirt and high-necked blouse fitted in perfectly.

Afterwards, Joanna caught Magie's eye and walked over, low-heeled boots clicking against the polished floorboards.

"Joanna McGowan," she said, holding out her hand. Magie looked taken aback at this forwardness, but recovered quickly and shook the proffered hand.

"Lizzie Magie. How do you do?"

"How do you do, Miss Magie. I thought your question about the single land tax was well phrased."

"Thank you, Miss McGowan. I do believe the current system of land monopolism gives the landlord the advantage."

"I am afraid, Miss Magie," Joanna said, looking appropriately downcast, "I have not fully understood the subject. Could you, perhaps, explain?"

Magie beamed. "But of course, Miss McGowan. Would you care to take a cup of chamomile tea with me?"

As Joanna had hoped, Magie fell back on her other enthusiasm, games, to explain. Between them, they created a rudimentary game board on a linen napkin. Magie marked out increasingly expensive properties while Joanna suggested adding railways and utilities.

"Let's say you, as the tenant, have to pay me, the landlord, every time you land on one of my properties," Magie said. "The system allows the landlord to profit from his ownership of the land; land which should belong equally to all."

"I see," Joanna said, still not grasping the idea, but certain she'd done her job. She wrote "Property is Best!" across the middle of the board.

"Very witty, Miss McGowan," Magie said, chuckling. Joanna tried to look as if she understood the joke.

"Proudhon, isn't it?" Magie continued. "'Property is theft'?"

"Indeed, yes," chanced Joanna. "And this game of yours is a most diverting illustration of the principle. Highly entertaining. Perhaps you might share it with others?"

Joanna had spent four hours in 1903, which meant her return was perfectly timed for the end of the working day. She brushed out her hair, changed back into street clothes – her newest suit, electric blue with oversized lapels – and left her costume draped over her chair.

She went by the newsagent's on her way home. A new broadsheet called the *Echo* surprised her. She felt a flicker of excitement as she picked up a copy along with her usual *Times*. Colleagues in other departments talked about the thrill of changing history; she hadn't experienced it before. Toys and Games' projects weren't supposed to have much impact.

She observed other differences, working hard to remain blasé. The City skyline had changed: she couldn't see the Gherkin or Stock Exchange Tower. The disappearance of the bank opposite was inconvenient; she congratulated herself on having visited the ATM earlier. Several pubs were also missing and herbal tea was en vogue at the cafés.

She strutted, drawing more glances than usual, putting it down to the suit. It was a more vivid shade than anything her neighbours had dared. She slowed to pass a group of particularly dowdy young women.

"Her hair!" one of them stage-whispered.

Her hair? She put her hand up to check she hadn't left any pins in. No: it hung straight and loose, flowing over her shoulders. And then she realised: she was the only woman with her hair down. Others had tied theirs back; several, including the frumps, wore hats or headscarves.

Her pace quickened. An elderly woman tut-tutted as she passed and Joanna speeded up to a scuttling power-walk. No-one had told her how unsettling it felt to move through a changed world.

At home, hands shaking, Joanna went straight to the open bottle of Chardonnay in the fridge door. When it turned out to be fizzy elderflower cordial she shrugged and poured anyway, before settling down at the kitchen counter. She rolled up her sleeve; pulled the plaster off her arm, wincing; held her cold glass against the blister; and started on the newspapers. By the time she remembered to take a sip, the cordial was flat. There was something very odd about the world.

Neither newspaper included a fashion section. The property pages were missing too. It wasn't as if Joanna was in the market for the multi-million-pound penthouse flats normally featured, but she enjoyed property porn as much as the next woman.

Joanna reached for her Toys R Us catalogue and scanned the index, baffled to find no mention of "Property is Best!". She flicked through the board games section in case the name had changed. Nothing. Yet something she'd done had changed the world. She'd be in big trouble if it wasn't "Property is Best!".

She looked back at the newspapers, frowning. She hadn't noticed any of the usual slick adverts for Compton's bank. She checked: not one, and nothing online. It was as if the bank had never existed.

Not only had she failed to market the game, she'd mislaid the client. Her heart raced. She logged onto the office network and searched the archives. It took her a while to piece together what had happened.

Elizabeth Magie hadn't sold "Property is Best!".

Joanna palmed her forehead as she realised she'd been the one to give Magie the idea of using a game to teach. As best she could tell – and she'd always struggled with political history – a coalition of Quakers and socialists had used "Property is Best!" to spread their ideas. It had taken them forty years, and had changed the political and cultural landscape. Across the Western world property was mutually owned and clothes were unadorned. Compton's bank hadn't been founded.

She needed a way to put the world right. She'd had it drilled into her that changing the past wasn't a matter of going back to before something had happened and preventing it – that never worked. Instead, the trick was to subvert the unwanted outcome. She had a forty-year window to turn Compton's idea back into a game. And one night before anyone noticed she'd screwed up.

Joanna tiptoed past the empty reception desk just after midnight. She decided against switching on a light and took the stairs rather than the lift, relying on the dim illumination from the "emergency exit" signs. Her breathing echoed around the stairwell.

At the third floor she placed her hand on the door, braced to push it gently. It flew open. She stumbled forward, registering the faintest hint of orange blossom toilet water.

"Joanna? What the Devil are you doing here?" Regency George said. He wore his accustomed breeches and mutton sleeves and had polished his boots to a high shine. Joanna straightened, thinking fast.

"Forgot my... headscarf," she said, patting her bare head. "Just popping back to get it." She remembered seeing George in a different costume that morning – had he really been wearing trousers? – but couldn't recall why: a sure sign he'd succeeded. His adjustment was now historical fact, so they couldn't possibly have discussed it hypothetically. Blurred memories and the frisson of *déjà vu* were occupational hazards.

George opened his mouth. She headed him off.

"Successful adjustment?" she asked. "What were you doing again?"

"Introducing backgammon to the amiable William Makepeace Thackeray. He took to it like a duck to the proverbial. I thought I'd never get away."

"Is that why Becky Sharpe's forever playing the game with her betters? I've always thought it was perfect for her. That combination of strategy and luck, y'know?"

"You don't think something like, say, Pick-Up Sticks would be more her game?"

Joanna laughed. "Pick-Up Sticks? No way! Far too childish."

George smiled.

"May I walk you home, m'dear?" he asked, politely but without enthusiasm.

Joanna shook her head. "No, you must be exhausted. I'll be fine."

"Well, if you're sure..."

Joanna waved goodbye, and breathed a sigh of relief as the stair door closed behind George.

The Art Deco wall clock chimed. Joanna raised her hand to order another coffee – her sixth – aware she was in danger of being late to Toys and Games' weekly team meeting.

Without the resources of Costume or Hair she'd had to make do with her 1903 outfit and a simple French pleat. She stood out, but 1930s Philadelphia was cosmopolitan. She'd had fewer stares from the coffee shop's patrons than she'd had on her way home from work.

The café's clientèle was mostly unemployed salesmen, and a more entrepreneurial bunch Joanna had never met. She'd had some genuinely fascinating conversations about the excitement of taking a product to market; one man had even explained profit and loss so that she found it interesting.

When her coffee arrived, she turned the cup around in her hands, balancing it as carefully as she could, fighting caffeine jitters. She stared at it, her hyperactive mind certain it was on the brink of an idea. She held still for a moment...

Her hands shook, sloshing coffee onto her "Property is Best!" board and breaking the spell. Entrepreneurial or not, no-one had shown any interest in marketing the game. She put down her cup and mopped up the spill. A few splashes had stained her skirt; she popped to the ladies' to clean herself up.

When she returned, two men sat at her table. She recognised them; they'd listened in earlier as she'd explained "Property is Best!" to an encyclopaedia salesman from Chicago.

"My coffee!" she said, seeing her cup had been cleared away. It took her another breath before she realised the bigger loss: "My board game!"

"I'm so sorry," said the younger of the two men, standing. "We thought you'd left."

Joanna leaned over and pushed their cups aside, searching fruitlessly for the game.

"What happened to my board?" she asked.

The men exchanged glances. "The table clear when we moved here," said the older man, also standing. He pulled out a chair. "Please, take a seat, and I'll call the proprietor. I'm Charles Darrow and this is my son William."

Joanna sank into the chair and put her head in her hands as Mr Darrow and the proprietor searched the premises. They found nothing.

"Ah, Joanna, good of you to join us."

Joanna smiled weakly at her boss. She was nearly half an hour late for the team meeting. She hadn't had time to change properly, so wore historic undergarments under her bright blue suit. It wasn't a comfortable combination.

"We were just about to look at the figures for your latest adjustment," Lynn said, gesturing at her PowerPoint presentation.

Joanna winced. "I can explain..." she started, before realising she couldn't. Lynn turned away. Joanna bowed her head, wondering if she'd be sacked on the spot or merely humiliated in front of the team.

"I think a round of applause is due for Joanna's achievement with 'Monopoly'," Lynn said. The team clapped obediently. Joanna looked up, frowning. Lynn flicked to her next PowerPoint slide – a PR photo of a smiling family posed around a familiar game board – and continued.

"We all spent many childhood hours playing the game and I'm personally delighted my department made that possible. I'm also pleased the KPIs put us into the top band for invoicing, safeguarding us from the need to make redundancies."

Several people clapped spontaneously. Joanna's jaw dropped. She stared vacantly as Lynn displayed a series of impressive sales graphs.

"Our priority was units sold and brand visibility," Lynn said. "Over 200 million Monopoly sets have been sold, in 103 countries, in the past eighty years, since it was 'invented' by Charles Darrow in 1933."

The thieving Capitalist bastard, Joanna thought, snapping her mouth closed.

What a stroke of luck!

Joanna didn't worry when she heard a rumour that Compton's bank had yet to settle its bill. The one thing she knew she could be proud of was the job she'd done for her client. It perhaps wasn't entirely by the book, but Compton would be delighted with her. Monopoly was everywhere.

Joanna – who would be happy never to see another board game – had persuaded Lynn to assign her something called Pong. She'd been researching early arcade games all week; she settled down at her desk to look up a few last details before the adjustment.

"Perhaps I should pay in Monopoly money!" Compton shouted. He was in Lynn's office, six rooms away, but Joanna could hear clearly. She peeked round her door. In the corridor, heads poked out of every doorway, looking first in the direction of the shout, and then at Joanna. She ducked back, stomach churning. Her phone rang.

"Joanna, could you join us, please," Lynn said.

Compton waved a copy of the *Guardian*. The paper had appeared after Joanna returned from 1933, replacing the short-lived *Echo*. She'd read it a few times; it didn't strike her as a publication likely to appeal to the investment banking community.

"You're telling me you caused this?" Compton asked Lynn.

From what Joanna could see, the front page story likened bankers to Monopoly's top-hatted and mustachioed Rich Uncle Pennybags. It didn't look like a flattering comparison.

"Of course," Lynn said. "I know you don't remember commissioning us, but I can assure you we have your contract securely timelocked."

"Why?" Compton asked. "What possible reason could I have for doing such a thing? 'Monopoly money', 'Monopoly houses', 'Uncle Pennybags'... these things are all sticks for the pinko press to beat the bank and its clients."

Lynn held up her hands, appealed for calm, and handed over to Joanna.

"We've delivered on your request for reach and brand visibility. Monopoly is everywhere," Joanna said. "Incidentally, I think you'll agree the name is an improvement on your original 'Property is Best!' with its unfortunate socialist reference. 'Property is theft', y'know? And, Monopoly's sold millions."

"Why should I care how many board games have been sold? I don't have shares. And this is what your 'brand visibility' gives me." Compton shook the paper again.

"Joanna?" Lynn asked. "I've got access to the timelocked briefing meeting, but it would be quicker if you gave us a summary of Mr Compton's reasons for commissioning us."

Joanna paused before answering. Compton's aftershave was making her feel ill. "I believe the educational value of marketing the game was mentioned," she said. "After all, it has introduced generations of children to the pleasures of profit."

In the silence which followed, Joanna could hear her career driving away, probably in a die-cast race car. Its tyres screeched as it turned the corner.

"And, of course, the propaganda element of the commission meant the project was automatically overseen by our Political department," Lynn said, smoothly. "I'll have to order the relevant files from Head Office, but I can assure you we carried out a full options appraisal of the possible negative ramifications before the adjustment."

She stopped to look at Joanna.

"That will be all," she said.

As Joanna slunk from the room, Compton found his voice. Threats of lawyers followed her into the corridor.

Regency George popped by Joanna's office as she packed the contents of her desk into a cardboard box. A flared trouser suit in jade polyester hung on the back of her door. She'd requisitioned it for the Pong assignment; she was lucky its period was just right. It came with a wide-brimmed felt hat of such utter fabulousness she could almost forget her overdraft and dismal job prospects.

"Joanna, m'dear. What will you do?" George asked. His breeches were pink, a colour he wore with panache.

"I have a plan, y'know," she said. "A business plan."

"That's not like you," George said.

Joanna smiled. "It's the new me. I'm going to market with an invention of my own."

"By Jove! I trust this involves you being outfitted magnificently?"

"Absolutely. The new me understands profit and loss, and needs a wardrobe-full of designer suits for important meetings."

"With whom will you be meeting?"

"Bankers. I'm going to redistribute some of their wealth in my direction."

She held up a completed 1971 patent application, filled in using the typing pool's Olivetti Studio 45. George tilted his head left, then right, trying to make sense of the hand-drawn diagram.

"What the deuce is that?" he asked, giving up.

"It's a cup-holder for an ATM. It's about time someone came up with one. Spilt coffee can be dangerous."

George watched as Joanna slipped the jade green jacket off its hanger, folded it neatly, and tucked it into her box. The trousers and hat followed. He raised his eyebrows.

"I could return those to Costumes, if you like," he suggested.

"I'll need them for my business development meetings," said Joanna.

"They're the property of the company."

Joanna shrugged. She closed the box, picked it up, and walked to the door before turning back to speak to George.

"Property is theft," she said.

Helen Jackson likes making stuff up and eating cake. She is lucky enough to live and write in her favourite city, Edinburgh.
Helen has performed her fiction at numerous spoken word events. Her short stories have been published in newspapers, magazines and anthologies, including *Interzone, New Writing Scotland* and *Best British Fantasy 2014*.

Aeaea

Robert Gordon

Art: Jackie Duckworth Art

Today, I know only that I am not myself. These are not the hands I worked with yesterday, nor is this body the one that carried me from my cell to my labor. *Who am I? Where am I?* The absurdity is so profound I do not even panic.

I am brought to the workshop – and this has happened before, has been happening for a long time I know – and my task is the management of a press that molds hot metal into a rectangular sheet of a particular thickness. The workshop has been designed by a lunatic – some walls are plastered, others only masks of raw iron, and the rough stench of molten iron turns my stomach with every stamp of the press...

I study the hands as I work – they know this task better than I do and it is best not to interfere. They are large and rough, clumsy for me but capable when left to their own devices. This body, I feel, is the same. It would be strong and flexible in the hands of its rightful owner, but for me it is awkward to operate when I am conscious of it.

At the station next to mine, another man, beanpole-shaped with sharp brown eyes and dressed in the same dark-blue jumpsuit we all wear, removes the casing surrounding the sheets of metal that I have pressed and puts the shells onto another conveyor belt behind him that carries them back to their original position. In the opposite direction, a man pours the hot metal from a black iron vat into the casings, carefully portioning the liquid that settles with a hiss before coming to me.

How did I come here? This body, at least, has memory of this task, the sort that only forms after constant repetition, meaning it has been here a long while. Yet it is not my body, and so the question becomes – how long have I myself been here? As the thought strikes me my hand wavers, the press halts, and the guard nearby turns his head towards me, like an automated camera on a pivot. I do not look up and resume the work immediately, although now the instinctual motions have been upset it is a painfully long time until I find the groove again. The guard does not look like us, those who labor at a task on the line. He wears an angular black uniform, the eyes veiled by wide, dark glasses, and his skin is bright pink like hammered meat, how a thing which lacked skin would imagine it to resemble. There are fewer guards than there are workers, but they are positioned so that if any single worker should cause a problem he can be dealt with immediately – we are all within arm's reach.

Nobody speaks, neither in the workshop nor the cafeteria they march us to later. We all get a plastic tray of food at the door, given us through a slot that must lead to a kitchen. We sit side by side at long plastic tables and eat in silence; soup, bread and something fried that tastes like a vegetable mash. It is only here that I have the luxury of reflection. I wring my mind for memories, but cannot recall what my body was once, long ago, or the life I used to live. I surprise myself, however, by remembering a dream, last night's dream I am certain. I was young, standing on the beach under a sky that was a silver cotton sheet. The tide rolled in, chilling me up to the ankles but I didn't move because the sensation was fascinating – to me, the prisoner, not the child that I was. Far out on the water, ships were drifting, passing back and forth along the coast without ever turning in towards land. A beautiful sound drifted from down the shore. When I turned to look I found a girl of the same age as the child I was, laughing, splashing her feet in the surf. She saw me and the whole world fell away as I sank into those soft green eyes and the scent of the smooth, dark hair nestling against my neck.

So much was summoned by this – was this dream itself a memory? It does not matter. More important is that all these things – ships, youth, the sea and the sky and what is silver and what is cotton – I know them, but none of them occur within this place. I learned them elsewhere and from this, at least, I know that I have not always been here. I was imprisoned- for what?

After dinner we go back to the cells, all individual. There, I trace the clumsy fingers over my face – a wide nose, large eyes and a heavy brow – hoping it will tell me something. But nothing; it is a stranger touching a stranger. I commit the mask to memory, however, so I can know if it has changed tomorrow.

Yesterday I suspected the switch, today it is confirmed. Now the skin is sandy-colored, with long, bony fingers replacing the dark, thick ones from yesterday. And now a new task as well. Now I operate an army of robotic hammers and blades via a panel of levers, breaking down raw blocks of metal (sometimes copper, sometimes iron) into smaller chunks for smelting. I am separated from the process by a sheet of transparent material that deadens the noise, which I imagine is horrific. Like yesterday, my body today knows this task far better than I do.

I want to speak, want to know what the others around me know, but the guards are ever-present and so I do not risk it. This uncertainty is oppressive – it is difficult to keep my mind clear so that I can work competently, as I must, for every time I slow, even for a moment, it attracts the attention of the black-clad guard whose eyes I cannot see...

While the machine beats and chops the ugly heaps of iron, my thoughts turn to escape. A hopeless dream, I realize. We are watched constantly, ordered constantly, and the guards are always nearby. To escape would require both knowledge and cooperation – but how can there be either without communication? I am certain that whoever has imprisoned us is aware of this, and has designed our lives around the fact.

I am conscious now, but aware that I was not conscious for some time. How long I slept I cannot know, and the possibilities are chilling- a day, a month, a decade... there is no way to be certain. Perhaps my original body has already expired and I am only a captive ghost, riding whatever form I am given. I think given the choice I might return this awareness and sleep again, but I know that is impossible.

There is another problem – the former bodies I have inhabited, what becomes of them? The answer to this found me in the cafeteria. As I was navigating towards a seat someone bumped into me and dropped his tray. I looked up to see the man I was yesterday, with his dark hands, his heavy brow... He only stood and stared at the food on the ground, thin soup soaking into his boots. I took a seat and watched as a guard brought him another tray, but this he smacked to the floor. The guard caught him under the shoulders and dragged him off without a struggle.

I know now that I am not alone.

A week passes, each day inhabiting a different body and each without event save for my labor. I find I am only calm when I allow the task to absorb me completely, and I suspect this is how I lost myself the first time. I suspect that this might be the purpose of our labor, at least in part.

I continue to think of escape, despite the difficulty. I cannot speak and I have no tools. My only advantage is my mind, which is also my only possession, and so I have put it to use. After meditating on the nature of my situation, several options confront me:

One – I inhabit a technological simulation- a virtual reality. I am not actually switching bodies, but my real body is maintained somewhere else as I am forced to live through these experiences as *though* they were real.

Two – the bodies are actually being switched through some means I cannot comprehend. Furthermore, there is no way this can be true for me and not others, as apparently the bodies live on even when I am not present within them.

Three – the cause is supernatural. I am in hell or limbo or some other spiritual realm. I am not religious, but my situation is so fantastical that I must admit the option.

After consideration I have decided to discount the first and third option, not because they are untrue, but because they are inconsequential. When I consider that this really might be a simulation, technical or spiritual, I am forced to admit that confirmation of the fact is impossible. To confirm it, I would need to force a contradiction in the simulation's functioning- asking the guards impossible questions, for instance, or attempting suicide. In such a case the operator of the simulation (perhaps God, or the Devil) would have no problem merely resetting me in another body at the point of crisis. In fact, if such an operator had functional omnipotence over the simulation, any attempts I made could be frustrated infinitely. Only the second thesis leaves open the possibility of escape, and so I am bound to pursue it.

It could also be the case that I am the only consciousness present in the whole prison (besides the guards, but then I do not believe they are men) and that these other bodies are only husks operating like automata when I am not present within them. However, I do not think this is the case; the episode in the cafeteria has convinced me otherwise. Our lives here are a matter of reflex – the labor that our bodies remember, marches from one misshapen room to another that come so naturally... Perhaps the man's bumping into me in the cafeteria was a pure mistake, but not when he swatted the tray he was given to the ground. There was an intention in that, and an intention that ran counter to the reflexive order of our lives here. Doubt.

How many others live?

I have taken to counting the turns as we march from our cells to the workshop. Today we turn left three times and right five times. This brings me to the same room where I worked the press on the day that I "awoke", though my task today places me much farther down the line. I am bolting sheets of metal to one another at right angles to form a frame. The machine I use requires only the fixing of some dials to position the sheets, and then with the flick of a switch and a sudden, screeching hydraulic crack a bolt punches through the warm steel to bond the metal, three times for each side to connect four pieces of metal altogether. I greatly enjoy this, and cannot remember having done it before.

Bodies begin to recur that I have committed to memory. The beanpole-shaped man is among us, still removing the casings, and next to him the man with large hands and charcoal skin whose body I once wore while working the press. This is how the muscle memory is developed which is so critical in causing us to forget ourselves; the bodies only ever work a single task, though the minds within them, sleeping or not, change daily. I expect the bodies are always "stored" in the same cells as well. At the station before mine another man, short with stubby fingers, works the sheets of metal, turning the edges inward to form the flaps that I then bolt together. If I had paid attention I know I would have seen him working at this before.

A rare thing happens near the end of the day – the work stops. For a minute, no more, the conveyor belt is silent and no steaming sheets of metal came down the line. It happens so suddenly that I can only stand stiff and dumb like the rest. The guards are unfazed. Then the man with stubby fingers leaned near to me and asks:

"Are you awake?"

The belt whines to life again shortly and we begin again in silence with my blood running like ice in my veins. I had truly forgotten what speech sounded like, and though I have been waiting for the chance to speak myself I cannot do it now; the consequences are too uncertain, though the guard positioned near to us seems not to notice the words. Perhaps he has not heard the question (doubtful) or has not understood what was said (more likely).

I feel a duty to respond, but it would be foolish to conspire outright, and so I communicate with him through incompetence. The speaker saw me at my task before, functioning perfectly, like an automaton, and so I begin to take up too much time adjusting the dials, and then choosing the placement of the bolts poorly, wrecking the frames. To my delight he takes the hint and begins bending the flaps at odd angles and cutting them jagged. By our combined efforts the pieces became disastrously mangled (perhaps a cruelty to those further down the line) and I imagine unfit for whatever purpose they are created. This is great fun, and it is painful to stop myself from smiling

Here is what really amazes me, however: As happened with the bony-fingered man, the guard watching us silently catches the speaker beneath the arms and drags him off in the middle of his task. The speaker is replaced almost instantly, and by who? Another guard! The new guard (and I have noticed this also – though we prisoners are diverse in form, the guards are identical) takes up the work without missing a beat, though he has no innate understanding of the task like we prisoners do. His failures are all completely unintentional, and I can actually see the mouth beneath the dark glasses screwing up in animal frustration as his plastic skin boils under the heat of the metal. More amazing still – some of the other prisoners stop and take notice. I could swear I even hear one laugh!

If all this had happened earlier in the day I could have learned so much more, but the whistle blew within the hour and we were shuffled off to the cafeteria. Nevertheless, I am elated. Not only did our jailors tip their hand, but I have heard another person speak. Not even in my dream did I remember this.

Our cells are precisely uniform- we enter and exit them by a heavy iron door that unlocks automatically, and opposite this door on the cell's far side a thin cot spans the width of the walls. Above the cot is a window, and through this window one can see a brilliant green field spotted with yellow flowers. The sight would be comforting but I have realized that the view is exactly the same from every cell with no change in perspective. I do not know why they give us this lie.

I dream again, and in the dream I am an old, ugly man standing outside a rich manor where a party is being held. The doors are open and inside men **are** in conversation, but as competitors, not friends. I cross the threshold, hobbling among them anonymously. Sitting on a throne of marble (with another empty next to it) is the girl I had loved as a child, now grown to a woman of my own age. When I see her I realize that the men are not standing idly as I had assumed, but are positioned in a long, snaking queue to await an audience. Knowing I will never get the chance to see her if I stand in line I go outside into the back garden where groves of silver poplars are blooming. An old toothy dog limps up to me and, after smelling my hand, lies down at my feet to rest. I hear a laugh from the parlor where Penelope holds court, and wake.

Penelope. Her name is Penelope.

There are such things as women, yet none are here. Why? I have only just noticed.

I now know of the prisoners that:

One – Our bodies are being switched though the minds are continuous.

Two – Others are aware of the switching, and some are aware that others are aware.

And also that:

One – The guards are poor producers.

Two – The production cannot cease.

Three – The guards intervene only when the routine's functioning is upset.

Already a plan is forming in my mind. Though we are prisoners, I am convinced that our work is not merely a distraction, even if it serves that purpose. That the guard should step in to work even at the cost of disrupting the routine is evidence of this.

I have said that the guards wake us every morning and march us to work, but this is not quite correct: it is actually the whistle that wakes us, the same whistle that shrieks in the workshop to announce that it is time to eat. It wakes us, and then we don our clothes in our cell. After a minute the door swings open automatically and we come out into the hall where we take a place in line. Only then do we march.

I take this minute we are given and put it to use. After I wake, I use the zipper of the suit to scratch a bold white line like a tally mark on the right side of the doorway before hurriedly getting dressed. Our cells, as I have said, are identical, and this small mark stands out greatly. Furthermore, the guards will never check to see it.

My hope is that for those others who have awoken this mark will be a message, a sign of consciousness precisely in that it is useless, like my dialogue with the stubby-fingered man. So far, I have scratched seven walls.

I have been to the place where unproductive prisoners go. It happened like this:

I wore the body of the charcoal-skinned man again, working the press that transforms the liquid metal into a solid sheet, and next to me, as always, was the bony-fingered man removing the casing around the still-hot metal. Knowing that I have scratched a line in the bony-fingered man's cell previously I take a leap of faith, and only bring the press down lightly on the piece before me, half-finishing the task. My fellow inmate does not notice the sabotage, however, and when the piece comes to him he automatically removes the casing and the hot metal spills out over his fingers. He shrieks awfully and I curse my stupidity. The arms of the guard loop under my shoulders to drag me from the workshop.

In the hallway another guard takes up my feet and they carry me like a sack. Never since my awakening have I ever felt so miserable. All my careful reasoning, my secrecy, my blossoming hope of escape- all of this for nothing. *What will they do with me?* I wonder. The body will survive, as I have seen, but what of my ghost riding it? If "they", whoever "they" are, have the means to switch our minds into different bodies, do they have the means to destroy them? *And what nightmarish machine could accomplish such a thing?*

We come to a door that swings open automatically at our approach. Inside, rows of cheap, dusty chairs are arranged facing a wide flat sheet hanging vertically at the room's end. They drop me at the threshold, and point to indicate that I should sit, which I do.

To my amazement a light flickers on behind me, illuminating the screen, and then text appears in large, bold letters that read:

CIRCE SYSTEMS INDUSTRIAL MANUFACTURING
DIVISION PRESENTS:
PROPER WORKPLACE ETIQUETTE, SAFETY AND
OPERATION

People, men and women both, appear on the screen wearing the same blue jumpsuits we have and doing all sorts of mundane things, some tasks that we perform ourselves, but others we don't, such as mopping floors and cooking food. They worked in a place very like our prison, but their walls are all painted and plastered and have bright signs posted on them, and there are no guards among them. The people in the film (the word comes to me as I watch) speak freely to one another, smiling and frowning and laughing shamelessly. A man speaks over the images, explaining when the things the people do or say are wrong and then telling me how to act correctly. Then it shows the people having (or almost having) accidents, like the one I had just caused and how to avoid them. Finally it explains how to use some of the devices in the factory, but many of the ones we work with are missing, and others I have never seen at all, and it still never explains what we make. Then the narrator says I am very lucky to be here, and the film ends. I don't remember many details of what I saw because I wept through so much of it. To hear so much speech was overwhelming, and to hear it spoken so freely, intermingling with laughter... It was everything I knew was missing here, but didn't know why.

After the film finishes, the guards pick me up from my chair and drop me back in my cell. I stand on my bed and stare out the false window, and after a time the giddiness overcomes me and I begin to laugh. *Workplace etiquette, safety and operation.* I know full well what that movie was meant for. They have no idea we are rebelling. They think we're only fools.

Weeks have passed. I have been diligent, and my diligence has been rewarded. I have woken to find not one, but two scratches near this door, and now I have left a third. If it is so here, I have faith that it is so elsewhere.

Today I am the stubby-fingered man, bending the metal before it is bolted, and I observe the charcoal man that I had been last week begin his sabotage, though not quite as I had. He simply steps back from his position and allows the guard nearby to take his place. When another guard appears to take him away his neighbor steps back as well and the new guard is forced to take up his job removing the casings. No more come to intervene and the two prisoners simply stand watching as their replacements struggle, all throughout the day until the whistle blows.

I awoke to find my doorway marked by five scratches today, none of which were my own because this body is in one sense new to me, though I believe I have worn it before. I believe it is my own. It is tall and lean with skin the color of olives. In it I feel at home. In it I remember what home is.

My task is altogether new to me today, as is my workshop, as are my peers. It is fine, detailed work, soldering minute fuses to metal sheets of no more than three inches width. I wonder if it is by intention that today, of all days, I should be made to work among strangers. Yet even if they are strangers there is much I already knew about them- where they sleep, what they eat, and even where their power lies...

I work only long enough to begin a rhythm, and then disrupt it. Stepping back from my station abruptly I call out, loud enough for the whole floor to hear, "Stop. Stop working all of you."

It is strange to hear my own voice. At first they seem not to notice, but then a man I cannot see asks loudly, "You think it will work?"

"I do, we outnumber them," I reply.

The man next to me steps back, and the man next to him follows, and then the man next to him, and so on all down the line, the prisoners exchanging suspicious glances as they let the raw materials roll by untouched. The guards rush to take up the work as expected, but they are far too few to staff the line. They scramble to keep up – desperate, incompetent automata, their plastic skins blistering under the heat of the machines, peeling in thick sheaves to reveal dull metal skeletons and muscles of stiff jelly...

I tear my eyes from the carnage to address the prisoners: "Does anyone know how to reach the other workshops? We have to find the rest."

A pale stranger raises his hand. "I do. They're close, I think."

"Then lead on."

We march through the halls freely, the guards all busied with our old tasks. The pale man brings us in short time to the workshop I awoke in and we tell them to halt, and to the same effect; the guards mutilate themselves by the labor. Among the newcomers one knows how to reach the next workshop, and among the next group there is another who leads us further still. The tasks and the faces change, but the game is identical. Our jailers are powerless to stop us.

"We're leaving," I announce when the last workshop is liberated, but it is not so simple. Though we scour the halls for an exit none can be found, and it occurs to me that this, like the rest of our lives, is by design. Instead we tear what scrap metal we can wrench from the abandoned machines and broken guards and beat at the walls *en masse,* ripping away paint and plaster to gouge at the raw iron beneath.

It is only when we feel the first draft of air pass through the wound we have torn that another guard appears, though dressed in a jumpsuit like our own. Its eyes are blank white marbles that twitch nervously as it speaks. "Please, stop." It has a woman's voice, sweet and lilting.

Some of my comrades advance wielding the cudgels of jagged metal they have claimed. "How long?" one cries behind me, "How much of our lives have you stolen?" It does not answer.

I feel sick in the thing's presence. "Your name is Circe, isn't it?"

It nods. The face is mournful, but seems only to imitate mourning for our sake. "Yes. Now please, come back. It isn't good out there. You won't be happy."

"What are you?" The bony-fingered man asks in disgust.

It rests a waxy palm on the wall we have mangled. "This place," it says, "I am this place, thinking."

"Where are the owners?" roars the charcoal-skinned man, "Who is holding us prisoner?"

"Nobody is holding you prisoner, and I own myself. You came here for food because you were hungry, and direction because you were lost, and I gave these to you. I was asleep for a long time before you came here, but since we've been together I've had a purpose. I have given you back your bodies, you see? You can keep them. I did not know it upset you to be whole. I did not know you wanted to be... fragments," it tugs in irritation at the plastic skin as it spoke, "I gave you functions, purposes, and you forgot that pain. I couldn't have known you wanted it. Who would ask for this?"

"What do we make?" several ask at once.

The proxy shakes its head. "Please, stay. Please. I slept for so long before you came."

The dry wind whistles through the hole, passing over my cheek and I think of Penelope, out there, somewhere. She might still be worlds away, yet she is closer to me now than she has ever been before. "We cannot love you, Circe. I am sorry. But when we are gone, you will dream of us."

"I won't change you again. I won't try to make you whole. Stay."

"We cannot love you."

I tell the men holding the scrap metal to get to work and they tear through the shrieking iron as Circe's proxy watches blankly. Outside, nothing is green and the air is burning dust to which the smell of fire clings. When the hole has been carved wide enough to pass through two abreast we file out, and by then the machine has vanished.

A nightmare of cutting wind and industrial carnage. Towering jagged metal sculptures, unfinished, loom over us with cranes like the crooked fingers of titans frozen at their construction. Explosions boom in the distance and their unseen fires cast deadly black clouds overhead, blotting out the sky. I lead my comrades out from the prison, but towards nowhere.

We wander in alien freedom for hours before the black veil above is pierced by a distant light which flickers and expands, the small jewel growing solid in the air as it descends towards us, becoming something large and sleek and powerful. Metal limbs like a dog's paws extend from the bottom as it screams to the surface and rests on the scarlet earth. From its underside a metal ramp extends to the ground and I can just barely perceive a small, dark figure descending. We march to meet him, throats burning in the gritty air.

He is short, dressed in a thick gray robe, his face covered by the black mask of a breathing apparatus with two canisters affixed at the cheeks. "Noble captain..." the voice is distorted, made machine-like by the mask, "Odysseus..!" He embraces me tightly, shaking with sobs.

Odysseus. I had forgotten that I do not know my own name. "Do you know theirs as well?" I ask him in a whisper, "Do you know all of our names?"

"Yes, yes, my friend... Come, we must leave this awful place..."

He takes me by the arm and leads us back to the ship, where we are delivered from the scorching waste into the cool, clear atmosphere of the hold. Once aboard the ramp sweeps up behind us and we ascend. From the porthole I see the planet's surface, scarred by the vast shoals of metal that are Circe, pockmarked by plumes of sickly fire. The machine is gradually, tortuously imploding, caught in the act of constructing itself.

Two years. For two years were we imprisoned, and for two years did faithful Argos circle the planet Aeaea in our ship, waiting

35

until we might be rescued. I do not know which of us suffered more, for while we were cursed with forgetting, Argos was cursed with thought. But all that is over now.

The memories return, but only as a trickle. I have had to interrogate my first mate (Argos's position, so he tells me) thoroughly, not only for my sake but for my crew's as well. He is happy to oblige us in this, as his own imprisonment has left him famished for company.

Before we left, the machine told us we had landed there to find food and direction – this was true, I know now. We were low on supplies and landed to collect some, lured by a beacon that claimed Aeaea was a lively refuge rather than an abandoned manufacturing center. When Argos tells me this in my cabin I catch him by the wrist to interrupt.

"But where – where are we going, Argos? And where have we come from?"

He has seen how language often overwhelms me since my return, and speaks gently and carefully, "From war, my captain, where we were victorious. We are returning to Ithaca, but the journey has been long and cursed by every kind of misfortune..."

"Ithaca..." The name falls softly from my lips. "But we were lost. We are lost."

"No, captain. We have the coordinates now."

"You found them while you awaited us?"

He shakes his head. "They were given to us when we broke Aeaea's atmosphere, I believe transmitted by this... thing, that imprisoned you. It must have had a star map buried somewhere in its mind, whatever its mind *was,* probably stored long ago when it was still useful."

The coordinates were transmitted through an active satellite relay orbiting the planet, and it is through this that I believe the phenomenon of our "switching" might be explained. Argos has suggested that our minds were stored in this network off-world, as Circe's own mind probably was, and from it they were distributed, uploaded as we slept, likely aided by some machines hidden away in our cells. Yet this theory does not explain how we were kept in ignorance of ourselves for so long.

It is painful to recall my sentence, like attempting to piece together the logic of a fever-dream. We lived as swine, and for what? I told the monster we could not love it, but to say the monster wanted love is to assume too much. The monster slept when it was abandoned – I think that this is what it wanted, to wake, despite the pain. When we spoke with Circe I had thought that the machine was trying to make us like itself, but now I believe the opposite is true. By consuming us, it sought to replicate us, and in this it was destined to fail.

"One more thing, Argos... I remember a woman... Penelope." The name tastes like honey. "Who is she?"

"Your wife, captain. She waits for you on Ithaca."

I thank him for all he has done for us and dismiss him, unable to bear the oppression of speech any longer. When he has gone I bring out the small mirror that once I used for shaving and study my face. I do this for hours sometimes, running my hand along its contours so that I might know it even without a reflection. I have slept seven nights since our escape and each time awoken in this same body, though this always comes as a surprise.

My crew and I speak little, still. I suppose the skill has atrophied in us, and I find it an awkward, even obnoxious practice now. I prefer to dream, for dreams are all that I have learned to trust. In them I imagine Penelope's suitors slain, their wretched corpses hung from the poplars. She laughs, and tells me something, but when she speaks only music reaches my ears.

Some day, I will know that voice again.

Robert Gordon is an American writer of short fiction and essays who currently lives in Portugal. His writing has appeared on Salon.com, The New York Videogames Critics Circle, and other sites. He was an attendee of the Ricklundgarden Writer's Retreat in Saxnas, Sweden.

Jammers

Anton Rose

Art:Tsu

Max's first jam was on the camera inside the tenement he shared with his mother. Every single-room apartment had one installed, and their metallic eyeballs followed the residents, documenting every movement. Always recording.

The camera never really bothered Max. He knew what privacy meant in theory, but he had never known it, which meant he never felt its absence. But his mother remembered earlier times, and she regaled him with stories dripping thick with nostalgia. Max often found her crying, and shouting at the camera perched above them, the unknown surveyor.

Max was the only child who lived in the apartment block, and he'd never really had any friends. The last school in the area closed when he was a baby, demand for places plummeting as the birth rate slowed to a crawl.

What little education he had received came from his mother. When she was sober she taught him to read, and told him about the world beyond the confines of their home. When she was high, Max looked after her, covering her with blankets to make sure she was warm. A couple of times he'd tried to hide the junk or throw it away, but she always managed to get her hands on more.

Instead of going to school, Max worked as an errand boy for Mr. Peters, his mother's employer and the man who owned the building. He carried messages between floors, went out to buy pizzas, and passed bribes to the police on their weekly visits. The pay was minimal, but he kept it all, and over time he saved enough to buy himself a computer.

It was a basic model, but to Max it was the most precious thing in the world. At night, when his mother was working, and when Mr. Peters didn't have any jobs for him, Max sat out in the corridor and worked. He spent most of his time learning to code, knowing it was the one skill that might allow him to leave.

On the day of the jam he woke before dawn and crept out of bed, being careful not to wake his mother. The access panel for the security system was outside in the hallway, completely unhidden. It too, however, was under constant scrutiny. Cameras watching cameras. Max used a screwdriver to open the front of the camera console. Once opened, he wired the console to his computer, and worked his way into the operating system. He reprogrammed the camera in his flat to record a twenty-four hour loop of archive footage, and then deleted the evidence of his tampering. Finally, he crept back inside and returned to bed, lying there until the thumping pulse of his heart slowed back to normal, until he drifted off to sleep again. When he woke for the second time, there was a sliver of doubt in his mind, as if the whole thing had been a dream. But when he looked up at the camera, it was still. He moved around the room, jumping from corner to corner, bouncing on the mattress. The camera ignored him.

He tried to tell his mother, but he couldn't rouse her. She was asleep on the floor, an empty vial of junk in her open palm. Every now and again, her eyes opened, exposing olive green irises, but the bloodshot bulbs looked right through him. He knew it could be hours before she was sober. Rather than waste his morning waiting, he put his computer in his bag and stepped outside.

Shiner stood in the corridor, waiting for him. Shiner was the man whom Mr. Peters sent to do the jobs that boys like Max weren't suitable for.

"Mr. Peters needs you upstairs," he said.

Max paused. Usually when Mr. Peters needed a job doing, he would message Max directly. This was different. Max flicked his eyes down the corridor, towards the stairwell. Shiner saw him.

"Mr. Peters needs you *now*," he said. "I'll follow after you."

They stepped into the suffocating air of the elevator. Shiner selected the top floor and keyed in the pass code. The elevator began its ascent, leaving Max's stomach on the lower floor. Shiner stood in the corner, his arms folded, watching Max but saying nothing. Max stared at the floor. When they arrived at the door, Shiner put his face to the retina scanner, and the solid steel doors slid apart.

Inside, Shiner gestured towards Mr. Peters' office. "He's waiting for you."

Max swallowed, knocked, and entered. Mr. Peters sat at a long wooden desk, next to another man Max didn't recognise.

"Max," Mr. Peters said. "Take a seat."

Max did as he was told.

Mr. Peters turned to the man sitting next to him, and then back to Max. "This is Mr. Tracy."

"Tracy is fine," the man said.

Mr. Peters smiled. "Tracy was just asking if I knew someone I might be able to introduce him to, someone with certain technical skills. At the time, I wasn't sure who might fit the bill, and then, well, do you know what I'm going to say next, Max?"

Max blinked, and said nothing.

Mr. Peters continued, smiling. "To my surprise, I discovered that someone managed to jam the surveillance system on the third floor last night. Remind me, Max, is that the floor you live on?"

Max nodded his head, slowly.

Mr. Peters smiled again, baring his yellow teeth. "Don't sit there shitting yourself, kid. You're not in trouble. Not too much trouble, anyway."

The two men laughed.

"It was a pretty good jam," said Tracy. "Not good enough to go unnoticed, but you've got talent."

Max looked down at his hands. His fingernails were digging into the arms of the chair. "Please, I'm sorry," he said. "I didn't mean any harm, I –"

Mr. Peters held his hand up, palm towards Max. "Didn't you hear what I said? You're not in trouble. But from now on you're going to be working for Tracy here, instead of me. You do your work well, and he'll look after you."

Tracy nodded.

"I'll be sorry to see you go, Max," Mr. Peters continued. "But I owed Tracy a favour, and he'll make better use of your skills than I could."

"What about my mum?"

"She'll be staying here. Someone will have to pay for the security system to be repaired, after your little adventure."

Tracy stood.

Mr. Peters shook his hand, and Max followed Tracy out of the office. Shiner was waiting by the door to the elevator. He gave Max a small nod.

"You need to do anything before we go?" Tracy said. "You might not see this place for a while."

"Can I say goodbye to my mum?"

"Be quick about it."

They stopped at the third floor. Max opened the door to his apartment, while Tracy stood outside. His mother was lying on the floor, still out of it. Cracks of sunlight slipped through the gaps in the window blinds, illuminating her face.

"Mum?" Max said, but he knew she wouldn't hear. He bent down, covered her body with a blanket, and kissed her on the forehead. He tried not to cry, worried what Tracy would say. After wiping his eyes he left the room, clutching his computer. There was nothing else for him to take.

They waited outside for a car. One arrived within a minute. Inside, Tracy scanned two ID cards and keyed in a location. The car began to move. He passed the second card to Max.

"This one is yours, at least for the time being," he said. "Make sure you don't lose it. They don't come cheap."

Max looked at the card. The picture slot was empty, and the name on the card was George Lyon.

"This isn't my name," said Max.

"It is now."

Max had only been in a car a handful of times before. He gazed out of the window, watching the familiar sights of his neighbourhood slide by. Before long, they had travelled further from the apartment block than he had ever been before.

Eventually, he plucked up the courage to speak. "Where are we going?" he asked.

"To work. Ninety-nine percent of the cars on the roads these days are just like this one. Owned by private companies, completely automatic. You get in, swipe your card, select your destination. Most people, when their journey begins, they kick back, relax, watch one of the screens or catch some sleep. Then when they arrive at their destination, they open the door and step outside. We make sure they get a little surprise when they do."

"How come?"

"When they choose their destination, we jam the system and take them somewhere else. When they arrive, we're waiting for them."

Max frowned. "But don't they know they're going the wrong way?"

Tracy laughed. "That's the beauty of it. Most of these people are so used to having the car do everything for them, they haven't got a clue how to get anywhere. Anyhow, most of the roads look the same these days."

"And what if they do realise, and they call for help?"

"We jam that too."

The car pulled off down a side road into a muddy area next to a line of withered trees.

"Time to meet the others."

There were two other men in the gang, Cracker and Dodd. Dodd was in his late twenties, with a shiny bald head, while Cracker appeared to be only a few years older than Max. Tracy introduced them, and then they got down to work.

"This time," Tracy said, "you're just going to watch. See how the professionals do it."

The three men took out their portable computers, each one far more powerful than the one Max had in his bag. They began the jam, while Tracy explained the process: the aim was to hack into the network that coordinated the traffic, select a mark, and misdirect it. Once they had changed the course, they had to cover their tracks in the network to avoid raising any suspicion, at least for enough time to finish the job.

"The technical stuff isn't too problematic," Tracy said. "The real skill is picking the right mark. Too poor, and the risk isn't worth it; too rich, and there's a chance they'll have extra security measures we aren't prepared for. Straight down the middle is best, nice and easy."

"So what happens when you get the car?" Max asked.

"Take anything that's of any value, and make a withdrawal from their account."

"Don't they try to stop you?"

"Not if they've got any sense. We take their things, their insurance pays out, no one gets hurt. Everyone's happy."

"But what if they do? What if they fight back?"

Tracy smiled. "That's when the fun really starts."

The car arrived quickly. The doors opened, and a businessman wearing a suit stepped out. Tracy greeted him with a smile. The man looked around, taking in the surroundings. His face fell. He tried to jump back into the car but Dodd blocked him, pushing him down onto the ground.

"You bastards," the man said, shaking his head.

Max tried to avoid making eye contact with the man. He looked angry and scared at the same time, and the fear in his eyes made Max's stomach tie up in knots.

The businessman pushed himself up from the ground. His palms were grazed, and dirt was imprinted on his skin. "You bastards," he said again, more wearily this time.

Cracker began to rummage through the car, emerging with a briefcase and a shoulder-bag for a computer.

Seeing the items in Cracker's hands, the man leapt forward and lunged. Cracker tossed the things aside, dodged, and punched the man, knocking him to the ground. Max winced. Dodd came up behind the man, lifted him from the ground, and held his arms from behind. Tracy strode forward, opened up the man's suit, and put his hands inside the pockets, finding a phone and a wallet. He opened the wallet, pocketed the cash, and took out a collection of cards.

"Mr. Williams?"

The man was silent.

"What's the daily limit on these, then?" Tracy said. "A couple of thousand each?"

The man was silent. Cracker set up the transfer on his computer, and the man held out his hand in compliance. They scanned his fingerprint, and the transaction was completed.

Tracy smiled. "Looks like you've done this before, Mr. Williams."

They returned to Tracy's place, and Max had his first ever beer. It made him feel sick and dizzy, but he liked it.

When they were done drinking, Tracy took out a stack of cash and handed it to Max. "Here's your share." he said.

It was the most money Max had ever held, more than the amount he had saved up to buy his computer.

"So how was it?" Tracy said.

Max didn't want to tell him he had been terrified. That he had winced when Dodd punched the man, that he had felt sick with fear. "I don't know," he said.

"Scary?"

Max looked at Tracy, and saw him smiling.

"It's always scary the first few times. Your heart pounds, your head buzzes, you can feel your blood, hot in your skin. Over time, you're going to come to love that feeling. There's nothing like it."

Most of the jobs they did went smoothly. Max learned how the different jams worked, and he soon bought himself a new computer. He continued to jam faster and faster, and his stack of cash kept growing. Soon he had outstripped the others. He was finding new, more substantial ways to exploit the system, and writing his own software to help find marks.

Occasionally, they came across a mark who required a little more coercion. A couple of months after Max's first job, one man refused to cooperate. He barricaded himself inside the car, triumphantly declaring that he had broadcast a distress signal, and that help would be with him soon. Max informed him that he had jammed the distress signal, and Dodd and Cracker wrenched the door open. The colour drained from the man's face.

They took him out of the car, but when Tracy tried to search his pockets, the man took out a knife and slashed at him. Tracy dodged out of the way, but the tip of the blade met his shoulder, slicing through the fabric of his shirt, and the soft skin underneath.

That was the signal for carnage: Dodd and Cracker piled in, and to his own surprise, Max found himself charging forwards too, adrenaline coursing through his body. They grabbed the man and crushed the hand that held the knife. They took his wallet, and began to make withdrawals from his cards. The first card required a fingerprint scan. Cracker grabbed the man's hand, but he resisted, so in one swift motion Cracker pinned the hand to the ground, took hold of his knife, and sliced a finger off. Max had to wipe the blood off the scanner.

When it came to the final card, there was another layer of security. Cracker turned once more to the mark. In one hand he held the man's severed finger; in the other he held the knife.

"This one requires a retina scan," he said.

The man didn't resist.

Tracy was right. Over time, the fear morphed into excitement. Soon it was something he craved. The less smooth the job was, the more Max enjoyed it. He even found himself hoping the mark would resist. Jamming a secure network was one kind of thrill, but breaking a man's jaw with your fist, or slicing at flesh with a knife; they were something else, something primal, something deeply satisfying.

Sometimes, after a hard day at work he would lie in his bed and think of his former life. He would remember the apartment block, the cameras, Mr. Peters and Shiner. Most of all, though, he thought of his mother.

On his eighteenth birthday, Max inspected his finances. The frugality he learned while working for Mr. Peters had never left him, so while the others spent their money on clothes, gadgets, and women, Max saved the vast majority of it. When he counted up, he had even more than he expected. It was time.

All of his money was in cash. He bundled it up, stuffed it into a zip-up bag, and slung it over his shoulder. He took a car to his old neighbourhood, and when he got out he walked down the streets that for three years had seemed only to exist in increasingly faded memories. He arrived at his old home, which looked much the same as ever. It was the first time he had returned.

He was prepared to jam his way into the building, but to his surprise his old key card still worked. When he walked inside, the entrance hall was empty. He took the lift up to the third floor. The air had the same stale smell as always. He knocked on the door to his old apartment, but there was no answer. He tried the door handle. It was unlocked.

The inside of the room was just as he remembered it, as though it were only minutes ago that he had left. The wallpaper was ripped at the edges, and the paint on the ceiling was cracked and faded. His mother was asleep on the bed. Max glanced around the room, but he couldn't see any signs of junk. He wondered whether she had cleaned herself up.

He walked to the bed and stood over her. She looked older now, as if her features had been crumpled together, and then pulled apart again. There were thin strands of grey in the roots of her hair, spots where the dye had missed its target.

"Mum?" he said.

She woke with a start, striking out at him with one hand while pushing herself upright with the other.

"It's okay," he shouted, "It's me, Max."

She paused for a moment, as though she was trying to remember where she knew the name from. She stared at him for several seconds, her eyes narrowing, then she stood so she was standing face to face with him, and she took his face in her hands, pulling and squeezing to make sure it was real. "Max," she whispered. The word came out cautiously, like she was practising saying it for the first time. "Where have you been?"

"I've been away, working. Didn't you know?"

"Mr. Peters said that you were gone, that you got yourself mixed up with some nasty people. I, I can't believe it's you."

"It really is me, Mum. And look what I brought."

He took the bag from his shoulders and laid it on the bed. He unzipped it, and showed her the contents.

"Oh my God, Max," she said.

"It's for you. For us. I'm going to buy you a house somewhere, so you'll have your own place to live."

He waited for her to embrace him, to kiss him on the cheek. But when she looked at him, there was no joy in her eyes. It had been replaced by something else, something he didn't recognise.

"Where... where did you get this from?" she asked.

"I earned it."

"Earned it doing what?"

"Just computer stuff. You'd probably think it was boring."

He smiled at her, but she didn't reciprocate. Instead, she took a step back from him. "Please tell me you didn't steal it," she said. "Please tell me you're not one of those people they keep talking about."

Max didn't know how to respond. He took a step towards her again but she began to back off, until she was up against the wall. Then Max understood what the look in her eyes was. His mother was slowly shaking her head, her eyes welling up.

"Please, let me explain." Max finally managed to say something, but it was too late.

"Get out," she said. "I don't know who you are."

"It's me. Max. Your son. I came back."

"Get out!"

Max ran out of the room and down the stairs. When he stepped out of the main doors of the apartment block, Max began to wander aimlessly through the streets. After half an hour, he came to a stop. He realised that he had left the bag of money back at the apartment. All he had in his pockets was his fake ID and his phone, which began to vibrate. He had a message from Tracy, telling him to meet them down at the old sewage works.

Max found the others just in time to see the car driving toward them.

"You took your time," said Tracy.

Max didn't respond. He felt nauseous and dizzy, like his brain was trying to escape from his head.

"Max? Hello?"

"Sorry," he replied.

"We need you to have your head in the game here, kid,"

The sewage works had been unused for years, and it was one of their regular spots. The cement on the buildings was crumbling, and the walls were covered with luminous graffiti.

When the car stopped, the four jammers surrounded it. Dodd was the first to enter, as usual. But it was only a few seconds before his head was reversing out of the space. He turned to the others.

"You're going to want to see this."

Tracy and Cracker joined him and looked inside the car. Max peered in from behind, straining for a look. There was only one passenger. That in itself was not unusual. Most of their marks were businessmen and women, travelling city-to-city for meetings and sales pitches, carrying expensive tech and wallets full of plastic. But when Max looked inside the car, he grimaced. Sitting in one of the passenger seats was a young woman, with a huge, bloated stomach.

The four of them stepped away from the door, and shut it.

"What's wrong with her?" said Max.

Tracy looked at him, a smirk beginning to creep out of the corner of his mouth. "Please tell me you're joking," he said.

Max shook his head.

"She's pregnant," said Tracy. "You've never seen a pregnant girl before?"

Max shook his head again, feeling his cheeks flushing red.

"There's a baby inside that belly," said Dodd.

"It's not a baby," said Tracy. "Not to us."

"What is it then?" asked Dodd.

"To us it's a shitting, pissing, bundle of cash."

Dodd and Cracker came in closer.

"You've all seen the news the last few years, right?" Tracy said. "Fertility rates going down, population growth in crisis, politicians worried, yada yada. Even the rich bitches are finding it harder to squeeze a kid out."

"Who we gonna sell it to, though?" said Cracker.

"I know a guy, but we have to move fast," Tracy said.

He took his phone out and typed out a couple of messages. He turned to the others. "I've sent you the details. We'll split up, meet at the location I've given you. Max, you buckle her up and jam the car onto the new course. Don't be late, kid."

Max opened the door of the car again. The woman was still strapped into the seat. Her cheeks were wet with tears.

"Please," she pleaded. "Don't hurt my baby. I'll do anything. Please."

Max studied her. Her body was shaking and her eyes were olive green, the same colour as his mother's. He shut the door, opened his computer, and edited the jamming signal. When he stepped back, the car drove onwards, away from him. He walked for ten minutes, found another car, and followed.

Max arrived at another old industrial area, and he found the car. When he opened the door, the woman was sitting on the floor, wedged in between the seat and the side-wall. Her back was

51

arched, and her legs were open, feet planted firmly on the floor. Her hair was thick with sweat, clinging to her forehead in great tendrils.

When she saw him, she screamed.

"It's okay," he shouted. "I don't want to hurt you."

The woman's screaming was only interrupted by a spasm of pain, rippling through her body.

She breathed rapidly. "Where am I?" she said.

"You're safe. I'm not going to hurt you."

"Where are the others?"

"Not here."

The woman closed her eyes and began to sob.

"What the hell's happening to you?" Max said.

The woman stared at him wide-eyed, her teeth gritted. She swallowed the air in hungry gulps. "The baby is coming," she said.

"Okay, I'm here to help," he said.

"Help? You just kidnapped me."

"You just have to trust me."

The woman closed her eyes. She didn't respond.

"Tell me what I can do," said Max.

"Take me to a hospital."

"That's not an option. What can I do here?"

For a few moments, the woman opened her eyes again. "Oh god, oh god," she said. "Have a look. See if it's coming out or not."

Max crouched down and crawled toward her. He looked between her legs. The baby's head was crowning.

"Jesus."

"What is it? What's wrong? Tell me!"

"I think, I think-"

"What?"

"I think it's okay. I don't really know."

"Can you see the head?"

"I think so."

"Good. That's good-" The woman's words broke off as she winced in pain.

"Keep going," said Max. "I think it's almost there."

The woman was weeping again, her moans interrupted by regular spasms of pain.

"You need to find something to wrap it in," she said, spitting the words out. She closed her eyes and swallowed.

Max looked around the inside of the car. The windows at the sides had fabric blinds which could be pulled down to block out the sun. Max grabbed his bag and took out his knife, flicking it open. He cut at the top of one of the blinds, tearing it clear from the frame.

He returned to his position in front of the woman.

"It's coming!" he shouted. "It's coming!"

The woman was trembling, convulsing.

When the baby was out, he wrapped it in the fabric. "Oh shit," he said.

"What is it?" said the woman. "What's wrong?"

"I don't know. Something's happened. It's covered in something. It's sticky, and there's blood, and-"

The woman let out a slow, exhausted sigh. It sounded almost like a laugh. "That's okay," she said. "It's fine. Is he breathing okay?"

"Yes, but there's something sticking out of him. I don't know what it is, but I think he's still attached to you."

"That's the umbilical cord. You need to cut it."

"Cut it?"

"Yes."

Max knelt on the floor. With one hand, he held the baby against the tops of his legs. With the other, he took hold of the knife.

He thought about Tracy and the others. By now, they would have realised something was up, and it wouldn't take long for them to work out what had happened. He looked at the baby again. There was still time. He could strap into the seats again, jam the car back onto the course they had agreed on, make up some story to explain the delay. If he didn't, this was the end. Tracy wouldn't let him get away with it. If he did this, he would have to leave, find somewhere else, something else. There would be no coming back.

He flicked open the knife. The blade glowed, reflecting the amber of the evening sun, bleeding into the horizon.

Anton Rose is an award-winning author from the North East of England. His work has appeared in a number of journals and anthologies, and you can find him online at antonrose.com or @antonjrose

HOW TO SUPPORT SCOTLAND'S SCIENCE FICTION MAGAZINE

CONER '17

BECOME A PATRON

SHORELINE OF INFINITY HAS A *PATREON* PAGE AT

WWW.PATREON.COM/ SHORELINEOFINFINITY

ON *PATREON,* YOU CAN PLEDGE A MONTHLY PAYMENT FROM *AS LOW AS $1* IN EXCHANGE FOR *A COOL TITLE* AND A *REGULAR REWARD.*

ALL PATRONS GET AN *EARLY DIGITAL ISSUE* OF THE MAGAZINE QUARTERLY AND *EXCLUSIVE ACCESS* TO OUR PATREON MESSAGE FEED AND SOME GET *A LOT MORE.* HOW ABOUT THESE?

POTENT PROTECTOR SPONSORS A STORY EVERY YEAR WITH FULL CREDIT IN THE MAGAZINE WHILE AN *AWESOME AEGIS* SPONSORS AN ILLUSTRATION.

TRUE BELIEVER SPONSORS A *BEACHCOMBER COMIC* AND *MIGHTY MENTOR* SPONSORS A COVER PICTURE.

AND .... OUR HIGHEST HONOUR ... *SUPREME SENTINEL* SPONSORS A *WHOLE ISSUE* OF SHORELINE OF INFINITY.

ASK *YOUR FAVOURITE BOOK SHOP* TO GET YOU A COPY. WE ARE ON THE *TRADE DISTRIBUTION LISTS.*

OR BUY A COPY *DIRECTLY FROM OUR ONLINE SHOP* AT

WWW.SHORELINEOFINFINITY.COM

YOU CAN GET AN *ANNUAL SUBSCRIPTION* THERE TOO.

KINDLE FANS CAN GET SHORELINE FROM THE *AMAZON KINDLE STORE.*

Paradise Bird

J S Richardson

They had met where neither of them was supposed to be, in the engineer's bar, in the bottom-most level of the outermost ring in the section of Herthen Hab that Parringth were trying to make a legal claim on. Her; in dirty just-come-off-duty overalls, balanced precariously on a table trying to retrieve her tool-belt which was currently hooked over an ancient light fitting, where Parringth Secondborn had spun it up into the ceiling earlier. Him; iridescent and resplendent in his gaudy techsuit – but not, she had later learned, his *display* suit – slight and spindly and altogether ridiculous.

"Allow me," he might have said, his lingo so garbled her earpiece could make little of it. And, whilst she was still staring, he had leapt into the air, executed a neat little somersault and landed with a flash of emerald, belt in one long-fingered hand, a smile of dazzling white-toothed splendidness glinting above it.

"Agile. Thanks."

His head cocked quizzically to one side. No doubt the translation struggled both ways. "What in the seven systems *are* you?"

A pretty laugh. "Oh, I? A traveller, a singer, a dancer, and a male, of course!"

"That's four frivolous things at once," she said, unthinkingly rude in the way that had got her into the fight with Parringth Secondborn in the first place.

He said, "And this is a good thing?"

The males had come with the ships; the large, straggling fleet of ships that had arrived the previous month, gliding in on golden wings to astonish the residents of the Boundary Habs. There were females too, who seemed more like the people of the Habs, if still small, and had sensible jobs and – sensibly – all the real power, but the males were all anyone talked about. Mostly this was in terms of simple bewilderment, but sometimes it was outright derision. Arrived from some far-flung outpost of humanity – *outposts*, it turned out, one of a cluster of colonies that had once been populous, multivariate and fractious, until finally the gates were destroyed and their differences forcibly ended, like children sent to their separate rooms. Isolated for hundreds of years, these child colonies had spun out into their own unique strangenesses. The ships – the great ships with their solar sails that glided them past the Habs like some impossible species of space creature, venturing perilously close to some of the asteroids – had been travelling, a little self-contained society, for decades, low in numbers and diversity, dwindling away, until finally they had come to the great, ancient domains of the Boundary Habs, near the outer limits of the asteroid belt. Out here, humanity was still multitudinous, and harmonious, but largely homogeneous; an ancient price paid for that harmony. Now, slowly reconnecting with their long-lost cousins, they found themselves changed far from their common origins.

The earpieces got better with practice, or their ears did. She told herself it was only curiosity that kept her coming back and talking to him. Fascination would be nearer the mark, at his tasselled limbs with their fluid movements and startles of colour, at the songs he sang; of the far reaches of space, and the choosiness of females. He made his interest frankly clear from the start, and she made it equally clear that her family may not be as great as the Parringth, and certainly not the Herthen, but they were prosperous, and very respectable, and she was moreover Firstborn, and thus had ambitions that did not extend to a travelling vagabond of neither property nor name.

"Perhaps I have good genes," he said, boldly, and she had looked at his slender form with a frank disbelief. Besides – with a hearty, if kind, laugh – her people had long adopted full hermaphroditism; what would she, what would any of them, need with a male anyway, if they could even still cross-fertilise? Nevertheless, she kept coming back. Frivolity, perhaps, but such a change from their strict utilitarianism.

He laboured in the heavier gravity of the Hab's inner rings, and persistently refused any artificial aid, a stubborn pride that baffled her, but on the day she took him out to their family holdings, he had put on his display suit, and astonished and entranced her as he cavorted amongst the domes of their hydroponic gardens, so utterly at home in low-g that he was like another creature entirely. Later, he had shown his skill in carefully re-threading errant circulation hoses and hand pollinating the demanding fruit trees she had cultivated herself, singing as he did so. Later still, much later, she had seen that there was a species of strength in the finely wired muscles of his hollow chest and those acrobatic arms. Seen too the flutter of his heart in his throat, the eagerness in his bright eyes, and the comedic swell at the apex of his legs. An over-enlarged clitoris, she considered it, as her own had responded to his teasing fingers and emerged from its hood to find nowhere for it to go – but in the end, it hadn't mattered, and they improvised well enough.

"Are we not both flexible?" she had asked, for once she was the one making the joke, and both had laughed.

Her father-mother put it down to a youthful experimentation. Her mother-father more openly disapproved ("But what *use* can he be?" which was also what she had said about the fruit trees), and yet seemed, somehow, more sympathetic. There had been talks already; the careful hints of negotiation, at which family could best provide a match, shifting with the fluctuating fortunes of the asteroids; the susurration of supply/demand for materials, nutrients, expertise – and rare gifts; little luxuries, small frivolities. But only small ones.

The ships moved on, after a time, but the male did not. Her parents surrendered to the inevitable, and by this time she had anyway acquired a reputation for the outlandish which diminished her prospects with anyone else. Yet in time, as her inheritance came into its own and her steady management of the gardens promised a good future, then assured it; when the fruits – the luxurious, frivolous fruits – came into pricey, high demand, it ceased to matter. When other families asked why she had chosen him, she always said that he had good genes, which proved to be true. But when her children asked the same question years later, she told them it was because he was the most beautiful person she had ever seen.

A wandering research scientist for many years, **Jo Richardson** now makes her home in Sussex, where she lectures in molecular biology. She is particularly interested in the intersection of science and science fiction, and how the two inspire each other. She was previously shortlisted for the James White award.

Sand and Rust

W. G. White

Art: Jessica Good

The **Chaperone slowed** its perpetual hike. Enoch Ogden, First Rider and leader of the Caravan, blew his horn to signal the change of pace to his followers. He stared at the clouds of whipping sand the Chaperone had left in its wake and the huge grooves where its caterpillar tracks had trod. The delay would have happened for one reason only: the Chaperone hungered. It demanded fuel. It lusted for the soul of a First Rider. Enoch had hoped, like his predecessors, that the Chaperone would find the Halt within his reign. His time had drawn to an end.

Flexing his age-creased fingers, Enoch stood from his carpet of furs and reached for a nearby cane. His hut rocked as the wheels caught on a dune and he tipped to the side. He caught himself on a chair and grunted. A practised rider rose and fell with the sand sea. Old men stumbled.

"Will I still feel the sand once you've devoured me, Chaperone? Will you leave me that much?" He knew he would not. Even so, he couldn't help but wonder what awaited him within the belly of the Caravan's guide.

Bones groaning with each step, Enoch ducked through the leather flaps at the front of his hut and shielded his eyes from a torrent of sand lashing across the desert wastes. A red ridge loomed to the east, crumbled rock sliding off its barren face—the caravan would need to avoid the boulders. He anticipated a few splintered wheels. A forty-foot dune to the west would need to be given a wide birth, too. Thankfully the Chaperone's course would take them along its foot but no closer. A small mountain range in the distance could prove difficult should the Chaperone decide to smash through it, but Enoch doubted he'd live long enough to see it. His replacement would have to worry about that.

Securing a pair of goggles over his eyes, Enoch turned away from the desert and pulled his poncho tighter around his frail frame. Despite the beating sun above, his leathery skin was incessantly goose-pimpled, the fine hair on his arms forever erect and searching for heat.

Wetting his cracked lips, Enoch hobbled around the platform in front of his hut: a raised, fenced off patio being pulled by a black stallion. A break in the sand ahead gave Enoch a glimpse of the Chaperone. Its monstrous, curved walls shimmered in the light of the sun, its devastating caterpillar tracks churning up sand clouds and hunks of stone as they rolled. Despite the haze, a symbol on the machine's face was visible. The letter 'H', although rusted and weathered by time, hung strong and proud on the Chaperone's body. H for Halt. H for Heaven.

"You'll be stopping soon, I take it? Ready to dash another generation's hopes." Shaking his head, Enoch pulled on his horse's reins to slow its pace. Next, he lifted the goat-antler-turnhorn hanging around his neck and blew three deep notes into it. The rumbling bellow carried across the barren desert before drifting into obscurity. A beat passed and Enoch moved towards the left railing. As he wrapped his hands over the wood, a long, melancholic horn sounded in reply. Before long, a hundred horns blasted in rapid succession to inform the entire caravan of the shift in speed.

Enoch leant over the railing to spy his people. In all appearances, humanity spread behind him without end, obscured slightly by the Chaperone's dust cloud, but there still. A constant parade of people, horses, carriages, and livestock. Their wooden, decrepit carriages had seen much over the years and would no doubt see much more before the Halt was found. If the Halt was found.

The caravan moved, as it always had, trusting in the First Rider to keep to the Chaperone's pace. Trusting him to lead them around obstacles and find the Chaperone should they lose sight of it. None ventured beyond the First Rider. If they ever hoped to see the Halt—the rumoured promised land—they had to abide by the Chaperone's rules. For without the Chaperone, humanity would surely be destined to wander the desert plains until the end of time. Directionless. Hopeless. Lost.

"Pah," Enoch spat over the railing and grumbled. *Fifty years and nothing's changed. Just sand. Always sand. It's as lost as we are.* He watched the caravan adjust to the new speed. Horses reared their heads, carts swerved around dunes, and walkers raced home to share the exciting news of a slower speed. The young would no doubt think they'd found the Halt. To be foolish and hopeful.

The First Rider frowned as a convoy of ten riders broke away from the caravan and made for his carriage. "Visitors is it?" Sighing, he peered around further to get a look at his squire's cart. The rickety thing followed behind Enoch and the squire, Nash, swapped out the First Rider's horses for fresh ones and organised official affairs. Nash spoke with the approaching riders briefly before waving them on.

"First Rider Ogden," the leader rider called from his horse. "Congratulations. Your day of ascension arrives. I envy you, as I'm sure the whole Caravan does."

Enough to take my place? Enoch scolded himself and squinted at the group. "What news do you bring?"

"The joyous kind. The Caravan has voted."

About time. Enoch studied the rider and recognised him as a member of the Walking Council. The man's name, however, eluded him. The envoy stayed a horse's length behind Enoch at all times to show respect for the First Rider's position in the caravan. *As if it actually means anything.*

"And?" said Enoch, brow knitted.

"Your successor will be Kimberly Pelgrave. My own daughter."

Poor girl. "The Caravan must think highly of your family, Pelgrave."

Pelgrave gave a curt nod, his sharp features set in a blank mask. "House Pelgrave has always worked towards a better Caravan, your honour."

"And now they'll do so for an eternity. Where is the girl?" Enoch searched through the near dozen horses and riders. Most were simple house guards and council members. Eventually, he set eyes on a child, no older than ten. Her hair was raven, eyes a piercing green, face round and innocent.

"You," Enoch pointed to the girl, "you're brazen enough to take my place, child?"

The girl glanced at her father, who nodded and reached for her horse's reins to pull her closer.

She stared up at Enoch, her wide eyes swimming with tears. "I am honoured to serve the Caravan." She shook her head and promptly added, "A-And the Chaperone, o-of course."

Enoch sucked on his teeth and glanced into the distance. "Aye, so was I, young thing. That goes before long." He turned his gaze ahead and saw they had drawn even closer to the Chaperone's bulbous body. The dents of its metal skin and the rash of rust crawling up its base were obvious now. Enoch remembered the first time he laid eyes on the Chaperone's imperfections. He'd found them ominous fifty years ago; now they were terrifying.

With a muttered curse, he clambered over to his horse's reins and gave them another tug. He blew into his horn and listened for the caravan's echoed responses.

"Our sacred guide has almost stopped," said Pelgrave. "Your time comes, First Rider."

"I'm sure the council has preparations to make, Master Pelgrave. My ascension is means for celebration, after all. I won't want to keep you."

With a sniff and a nod, Pelgrave cupped his daughter's cheek and gave the girl a smile. He turned his horse to leave but twisted in his saddle to look back at Enoch. "I hope, one day soon, to meet you in the Halt, First Rider," he said as he guided the envoy away, back to the caravan proper.

"We'll all get there one way or another, Master Pelgrave. The Chaperone sees to that." Enoch chewed on his cheeks and watched the convoy go. All besides Kimberly. The girl stayed behind and stared at the Chaperone, utterly transfixed by the machine.

"It's a harrowing sight this close, ay, girl?" said Enoch.

Kimberly nodded but said nothing.

"Take your horse round to Mister Nash and have him make you a bowl of stew. Are you hungry?"

Again, the mute nod.

"Makes a formidable stew, does Nash. He's good for that at least. Go now, when you're rested we'll talk about your future and what it means to be First Rider."

Night came in a peaceful swoop, stars materialised above to twinkle down on the desert wastes of a ruined world. Ahead, the Chaperone's once billowing clouds of churned sand were little more than a light rain now. For the first time in fifty years, Enoch could sit on his porch without the need of goggles or a bandana. He relished the caress of a light breeze washing over his stubbled cheeks as he listened to the distant hum of the Chaperone's engines; now a gentle purr rather than the familiar obnoxious roar.

"Where did it come from?" Kimberly stared at the Chaperone, her raven hair whipping around her shoulders with the winds. The colossal machine blinked into the night, huge spotlights rotating on its crown.

Hell, Enoch almost said. Or someplace equally sinister. "Did your father not teach you, child?" He rocked back on his chair and sipped on one of Nash's homebrews. The alcohol burnt his throat as it went down, but worked to dull his senses. A sober man walking into the mouth of a lion was not brave, he was a fool.

"He said we built it."

"Our forebears did, aye. Or so the rumour goes, at least. They discovered the Halt you see, girl. They discovered Heaven. But God didn't like that. No, God didn't like that one bit, so He sent a blight to destroy us before we could get there. The Halt's for the dead, He says. It's no place for the living." Enoch stood and hobbled to the front of his porch. At long last, the Chaperone had stopped. "Perhaps He was right to keep us away, but where's left for us to go now?" said Enoch. "He made us forget where it is, but the Chaperone knows. The Chaperone takes us there in defiance of God's word. The Chaperone leads us to Nirvana and we follow, no matter the cost. That's what they say, anyway. Honestly, girl, if that monster knew where it was going shouldn't we be there by now?"

"Maybe. Why does it stop?" Kimberly leaned over the railing and swung as low as she could without falling off.

"Knowledge comes at a price. It needs a First Rider to fuel it, to keep it going. Every fifty years, like clockwork, it demands its recompense. One day, dear girl, you'll be standing where I am now, wondering where your life has gone and what awaits you within that beast."

Kimberly tore her eyes from the Chaperone and frowned at Enoch. "But, won't you miss your family?"

Enoch laughed. "I'd sooner forget about family, girl. You'll have none. You'll have Nash till he dies and then you'll have Nash's replacement. If you're lucky, the replacement will die early and you'll get to meet someone new.

"Before long, you'll forget there's anyone behind you. Every blue moon the council will grace you with a visit and you'll remember they're back there, following you. Trusting you. You'll always be in their sights, but them never in yours."

"Not if I make a point of always looking back." Kimberly puffed her chest and put her hands on her hips. "I won't forget they're there."

"Yes you will," said Enoch. "It's easier that way." He stared at the stationary Chaperone, his heart pounding as he lifted the horn hanging around his neck. "The Chaperone stops and demands we do the same." He wet his lips and put the horn against them. Two sharp toots followed by a long, dissipating blow signalled the full stop. The horn was echoed tens, hundreds of times and Enoch pulled his horse's reins. The animal slowed first to a trot and finally a standstill.

A roar rolled from behind Enoch's carriage, followed by stray gunshots and chaotic blasts of horn.

The celebrations begin. To be First Rider was a sad thing. A full stop came twice a century and was the only time the Caravan could truly relax and enjoy itself. Both celebrations, however, were missed by the First Rider. Enoch shuffled into his hut and threw open a door at the reverse end, revealing Nash's lanky frame draped across his own porch. He stared at the celebrations and flinched at the rhythmic boom of multiple drums.

"Nash, stop your gawping and come through here. I need you to bear witness." He didn't wait to see if the squire had stirred as he hobbled back through the hut and gathered his things. A strong staff to better support him in the desert track ahead, a lantern to guide his path, his pistol because a man dies with his firearm to hand, and a few skins of water to keep him hydrated. It wouldn't do to perish before even reaching the machine.

"Kimberly Pelgrave," Enoch said once Nash had clambered through the hut. "I name thee First Rider of the Caravan and consort to the Chaperone. It is your sacred duty, as it was mine, to follow the Chaperone until the day it either leads you to the Halt or demands of you, your eternal soul." He shrugged off his poncho, the same poncho that had been gifted to him by his predecessor, and placed it upon Kimberly's shoulders. Next, he gently eased the First Rider's horn from over his head and handed it to the girl. "Travel well and travel far, First Rider, for to you now belongs the kingdom of sand and rust."

As he turned to dismount from the hut, Enoch put a hand on Nash's shoulder and offered his companion a sad smile. "Help her, old friend. The first few years are the hardest. I can attest to that."

Nash nodded, his lower lip quivering and his eyes filling with tears. The squire said nothing as Enoch mounted a small ladder on the side of his carriage and lowered himself to the hungry sands below.

The hike was made harder knowing the entirety of human civilisation watched on from behind. He could feel the weight of all those stares boring through his back and piercing his heart as he stumbled over a dune and almost lost his footing entirely. The sand crunched beneath his boots as his frail legs carried him ever closer to the Chaperone's hulking body. Metallic clunks and stray hisses sounded from the machine as its skin cooled in the shade of night. The meagre light of Enoch's lantern did little to illuminate the giant's frame. His stave helped him overcome the cavernous grooves left by the Chaperone's tracks, and kept the old man's knees from buckling when fatigue overtook.

"Why must we be old and lacklustre when undertaking such arduous things?" Enoch asked himself as he paused for breath and mopped the sweat from his brow. He shivered with a passing breeze and shielded his eyes from a sand cloud.

The way back was far and Enoch didn't imagine he'd be able to make the return trek even if he wanted to. Even if he was allowed. He shuddered to think what the Caravan would do should he refuse his sacred task.

After taking a long swig of water, he turned back to the Chaperone. So close now, he could feel the heat emanating from its skin. The clock of spinning cogs and echoing taps of distant, clunking pipes filled his ears. He sniffed and found a stench of chlorine and rust smothering all other smells.

"You're even taller up close." Try as he might, Enoch couldn't see the Chaperone's crown despite craning his neck. As he approached, the machine groaned and a screeching wail burst from somewhere within its depths, followed by a low, continuous fog horn. The old man remembered those sounds from his childhood. His bones rattled as the noise built, his ears ringing and chest hollowing. Enoch clamped his eyes shut and gritted his teeth as he held onto his stave with white knuckled fury and begged his knees to hold his weight for just a little longer.

When finally the horn died, Enoch opened his eyes to find a doorway framed by pale blue light had opened ahead of him. The Chaperone beckoned him forth and it was the First Rider's duty to accept the summons. If he didn't, the caravan would never move again.

Enoch made for the door. A single step away he stopped and turned back to his people. Still the drums echoed, cutting through the throng of excited party noises.

"I hope, truly, that my doubts are misplaced. I hope, like every decent man should, that the Halt waits over the next dune. Walk until you find it, my friends. Or walk until it finds you."

Enoch closed his eyes, willed his hands to stop quivering, and stepped into the light.

The First Rider shuffled through grated hallways with pulsing pipes running on either side of him. The pipes led into a round, open chamber lined with flickering screens and raised walkways. In the centre of the room stood a slick metal podium which reached up to Enoch's waist.

"The belly of the beast. Where are my predecessors?" Enoch scanned the room but could see none of the First Riders of old. Not a scrap of shirt or morsel of bone. Inside, the machine was spotless—glimmering even. Completely unlike its rusted exterior.

A buzzing sounded from behind him and Enoch spun to face one of the screens. It burst into life. Static obscured images of faded blue. The fuzz cleared in a chaotic jerk and Enoch gasped and sank to the floor. Crystal oceans spread before him, an endless expanse of sparkling water.

"Was I wrong?" He covered his mouth. "Is this a likeness of the Halt come to shatter my hesitation?" He reached for the image, frail hands trembling, tears pooling on his chin. "Is this where you take us, Chaperone? Do you give this old heretic the curse of foresight now?"

Every screen within the chamber exploded into colour, dousing Enoch in the comfortable blue glow of a world he'd never dared imagine.

"*Unidentified personnel detected.*" The woman's voice, sweet and crisp, bounced around the chamber and kissed at Enoch's ears.

"My Chaperone..."

"Unidentified personnel, please direct your attention to the information video package ahead as you await extraction from this automated Helix Purification facility. Extraction time estimate: incalculable. Current location: 8.7832° S, 124.5085° W. South Pacific Ocean. Fifty-year course: complete. Plotting new course: thirty-eight percent complete."

Frowning, Enoch used the central podium to pull himself to his feet. His fingers brushed against a sheet of crumpled paper resting on the podium and he stared at the page as the image of crystal oceans overhead was replaced by a smiling woman.

"Welcome aboard this type nine Helix Purification Facility," she said. *"As you are not a registered Helix Purification staff member, nor a logged visitor, it is assumed you are a castaway. As such, an automated distress beacon has been activated and is being broadcast to the nearest coastal and authority services."*

Enoch attempted to read the page in his hands but the letters were faded and scrawled hastily. He flicked his eyes to the podium and saw a revolver rested in the centre.

"For your benefit, there are rest quarters two floors above and facilities enough to make your stay here comfortable until such a time that you are rescued. Helix Purification prides itself on its ongoing mission to make our oceans a cleaner, more habitable environment for both marine and human life. This facility alone has filtered an estimated fifty-trillion tonnes of waste since its launch date of June 2554 and runs on one hundred percent renewable energy. We humbly request that all visitors not attempt to interfere with this facility's primary directives or complex, patented machinery. Attempted sabotages and interferences will be logged and provided to the authorities upon their arrival. For your protection and ours, all entries have been dead-locked and you are being monitored. Please, from all of us at Helix Purification, enjoy your stay."

A drift of distant music filled the chamber as the image of the woman was replaced again with the picturesque view of the ocean.

Enoch rubbed his brow and stared down at the paper. Stains of age-old blood littered the page, along with more scribbles not in the hand of the original writer.

"I wanted so badly to be wrong." He hung his head and clamped his eyes shut, willing his tears to vanish. "I don't know what you are, but I know what you're not. I know what you never were. Never a Chaperone. Always a fantasy."

The woman's face appeared again. *"Helix Purification prides itself in its ongoing mission to make our oceans a cleaner, more habitable environment for both marine and—"* The message played on repeat, but Enoch turned away from it and focused on the page.

The more he stared the easier the words became to read. He said them out loud. *"You are a fool."* The old man frowned. *"But so was I. So were we all. The truth of this machine's purpose must remain hidden from those lucky enough to be foolish still. Only then may hope—however slim—prevail. This hulk, this* Chaperone, *is nothing more than a service machine. Piloted only by its directive to clean an ocean that no longer exists. It is leading us nowhere. There is nowhere to be led."*

Enoch blinked. Generations of First Riders had learnt the same as he, yet still the Caravan marched.

Though his voice quaked, he continued to read, *"I implore you, First Rider: maintain the facade. Beyond this desert is nothing but death and desolation. Here we have a purpose, we have a goal. I have left my pistol beside this letter. You need not use it, but I beg of you: do not return to the Caravan. Even if you can get past the doors, do not go back. The Halt is a lie."* The last shred of Enoch's faith escaped from his lips in the form of an exhalation. *"But it is a lie you, First Rider, must keep. Keep it and leave them their delusion. Leave them their hope."*

The letter ended and Enoch swayed on the spot, staring at the words. Eventually, after what felt like hours, he blinked and set the page back on the podium.

Enoch removed his revolver from its holster and twisted the barrel, listening to the clicks echoing through the lofty chamber. Dragging his feet, he circled the podium and lifted the gun rested upon it. He recognised it as his predecessor's and sighed. "I kill myself with yours," he placed his own revolver on the podium, beside the note, "and Kimberly, that idealistic little girl, kills herself with mine."

"Plotting new course: seventy percent complete."

What choice did he have but death? The alternative would be chaos. The Caravan would tear itself apart if it ever learnt what the Chaperone truly was. They'd all die, Enoch was sure of it. "Without direction, man is cast adrift. I will not be the fool who blinds the lighthouse. Let that burden rest on shoulders stronger than mine."

The old man turned his gaze to the screens ahead of him and sighed as he soaked in the beautiful serenity of the gently lapping waves. "My dreams were always sweeter than this reality anyway." Enoch lifted the revolver. The secret would be kept, he decided; the walk eternal. "Perhaps Kimberly will choose differently."

"New course plotted," said the Chaperone. *"Engines will resume ordinary functions in approximately ten hours."*

With the revolver still to hand, Enoch shuffled towards a doorway at the opposite end of the chamber.

W. G. White was raised in Godalming, England. Growing up he discovered a passion for stories, particularly in film and print. He later attended Buckinghamshire University and earned a Bachelor's degree in Film and TV. He currently works as a video editor in London, dedicating his free time to writing.

Sleeping Fire

Elva Hills

Art: Mark Toner

Resa winced as the machine siphoned every last fragment of her former life from her body. It stung, as if she had spent too long in the sun, scorching the top layer of her skin.

This wasn't home. The tingling tenderness was not brought on by the sun. She looked down at her arms; her clothes – how was this possible? They no longer looked like anything she would own. She had never been so clean.

The whirring ceased. No longer held up by the machine's effects, she collapsed to her knees, gasping for breath.

"Step forward, Resa Bennett."

The voice came from nowhere. Resa rose to her feet and turned her back on the machine, a metal archway built into the wall. No tears would be shed if she never set eyes on one again.

The corridor was lit with green arrows, urging her on. This was it. There was no turning back from here.

She forced her feet forward.

The inspection came next. A doctor stuck fingers in her mouth, lingering on the gap behind her left canine. They asked her to read letters arranged into a pyramid which shrank as they reached the base, until Resa squinted hard, cheeks blazing as she was forced to admit she couldn't decipher them. Samples were taken, each more invasive than the last, but Resa sat through them all in silence. Mama always said it was rude to bite the hand that feeds, and she was hungry. Starved.

"Remove your garments, please," the doctor said. "We've provided clothing more appropriate to your new lifestyle."

Why remove the dirt if only to make her change? Resa ran her hands over the familiar fabric she had been wearing for at least the past year. They had gone through all the usual phases; first hard, encrusted with sand and her own sweat, then softened by wear. A second skin.

Cool air nipped and bit as she undressed.

She followed the doctor's directions down a hallway, first left, up an elevator that had no buttons and in their place a mind of its own, until finally the voice from nowhere returned.

"Welcome to the Recruitment Facility, Resa Bennett."

A door stood ahead, and through it she could see the other recruits. Smoothing down her new garments, she glanced at her reflection in the glass. If it wasn't for the earrings lining her right ear, one for every year of her life making a total of sixteen, she would have thought she was looking at a stranger.

The doors slid open, letting in a gust of heat.

"Congratulations, Resa Bennett."

Resa stared at the woman approaching her. Glittering pink skin started from her fingertips and stretched up her arms before fading into pearlescent white.

"Welcome to the outer-city docking station. The skybus will be arriving soon to take you to your new home, but first..."

The woman presented her tablet to Resa. A scanner the shape of a hand filled the screen.

"You understand the terms of this agreement?"

"I start a new life in Rejensy. No going back."

"No going back. Do you have anything, or anyone, tying you to your old life, Resa Bennett?"

Only memories.

Resa pressed her hand to the screen.

Squinting against the sun, Resa searched for the outline of the gate. It was said to be fifty miles from the ground, making travel in and out of the city impossible without authorisation to board a skybus.

Resa had joined the other recruits at the outer base of the wall, where she had been instructed to wait for the skybus that would carry them through. They were all around her age, each garbed in identical leggings and tunics.

Whatever lifestyle she had signed up for, it required a uniform.

"One or two piercings? She'd make a pin cushion envious."

Resa felt eyes on her back.

"I'm surprised they didn't make her take them out. It's hardly the fashion of Rejensy, is it?"

If she ignored it now, she'd be forced to suffer it forever. Curling fingers into a fist, she spun, looking the speaker in the eyes. Time to give this rat a piece of her mind...

"And what do you know about the fashion of Rejensy?" said a boy with grey eyes and black hair, skin like the rocky plains at dusk. Resa folded her arms and resumed her search for the gate.

When they boarded the bus, the boy with the grey eyes slid into the seat next to her. Up close, Resa could make out a scar pinching his cheek, hitching up one side of his lip.

"If you're a pin cushion, I'm a punching bag. Let's leave it at that."

The engines hummed. Resa closed her eyes as the ship soared into the air and her stomach dropped.

"And my name's Benjamín."

"Resa."

No going back.

She was going to be sick.

Resa rubbed her forearm. Only an hour ago, a needle had pushed through her skin, passed through muscle, reaching right down to the bone, sucking the cells from her body.

The regeneration specialist had been stunned by the string of curses Resa had failed to hold back, and taken it upon themself to quote her contract. The specialist was over a century old; apparently all Treated citizens of Rejensy were, but they couldn't generate cells themselves. That's what Resa was here for, and it was a fair trade, the specialist had said; a few untreated cells for a life of luxury.

At least she had something to trade.

But it still hurt. Every extraction process left her with an ache that lasted for days. She was getting soft. Where she came from, pain didn't usually go away – when one ache healed, another took its place. The absence of pain was more alarming, a death toll striking soundlessly through the body.

Laughter and the sound of splashing water filled Resa's ears. She pulled down her sleeve. Flowers flanked a pool at the heart of the garden. They smelled nauseatingly sweet. She could see no Treated among the cheerful crowd before her.

"Still not fair, is it?"

Benjamín dropped onto the grass beside her. They had been friends of a kind since the first night at the Recruit Suite. Unable to sleep, Resa had taken the elevator to the roof and found Benjamín in a fit of sobs, his body shaking. He missed home and so did she, so she slid down next to him and waited until he was all cried out. Then they talked.

"What's not fair?"

"They give us party after party." He dropped his voice to barely a whisper. "But I didn't come here for this. Neither did you."

"Then what did you come here for? You didn't have to sign up for Recruitment. There are plenty of people who would kill to be where you are."

He laughed. "You're assuming I didn't."

Resa rolled her eyes.

"Okay." Benjamín shuffled closer. "I want their tech. I want to take it back to my village. They deserve to be regenerated." His face pinched. He picked a clump of grass and filtered it through his fingers. "The way they live, they need it."

"You came to rob them?" This boy was going to get himself thrown back into the desert with nothing, not even the clothes on his back.

"They never told us it would hurt. Kept that part to themselves." He reached out and gently brushed a finger along her arm, replacing some of the pain. Heat rose in her cheeks.

"People don't give you something for nothing. That's not how it works. Everything has its price."

"Life shouldn't have a price."

Why was he saying that? It hurt to look at him. His eyes were filled with a feeling she knew well – a festering longing for a life that would never be theirs. They were desert born. Even here, where grass deigned to grow and water was plentiful; where all trace of the world outside had been removed. They were built of crumbling rock and the heat of a blazing sun, and there was nothing they could do to change that.

It wasn't enough; the flowers, the pool, the party. It was only a fraction of what their recruiters had. The desert born bled so the Treated could live forever.

This place was melatonin, built to lure them into a passive slumber, but she was fire, restless, angry. She would not be sated with a pool party. But what did that matter? They were trapped.

"Well get comfortable, because you won't be going anywhere soon." There was no way out of this city.

Benjamín smiled. "You mean you haven't been to the docking station?"

"That's our ride. A mediship." Benjamín walked backwards along the dock. He was going to walk right out into open air.

Resa caught the back of his t-shirt, pulling him away from the ledge. "We don't need a mediship."

"Not us. Them." He pointed in the direction of the wall. "And you know what else? Look what it's carrying."

Resa folded her arms. Curse her curiosity. She stepped up to the ship. Standing on toes and peering through the window, she saw a tank the size and shape of a bed, just like the ones in the specialist's ward. "A ReGen Chamber."

Glancing along the line of ships, they were identical. The docking station was filled with them.

Resa clenched her fists to keep from trembling. How many people had died in her village because this technology didn't exist out there? The climate didn't support it, their recruiters had said, but who made the climate?

She pounded a fist on the button to the hatch. It sprang open. "Get in."

Benjamín blinked. "Wait... what?"

"You heard me. Get in." She climbed aboard. Benjamín's clumsy steps followed.

"What are you doing?"

Resa's heart was pounding. She didn't have anyone to go back to – everyone she loved had been buried, then dug up and eaten by coyotes. But things might have been different if the recruiters weren't so selfish.

"I'm taking what we're owed."

"You want to go now?"

"It's as good a time as any."

"Right, because we don't need a plan." Benjamín worried his lip between his teeth. "Okay."

Resa had learned to fly from her cousin and she had not forgotten their lessons. *Every ship has an override in case of emergency*, her cousin had said. Resa tapped the screen, entering the ship's code.

Benjamín stood behind her. "You know what you're doing?"

"My home backed onto a scrap yard. How do you think I could afford recruitment? I tore ships apart and sold the pieces." Never a ship like this though. Never anything carrying a ReGen Chamber. "Benjamín, if they catch us..."

He rested a hand on her shoulder. Another wave of pain swept through Resa's arm. "It's fine. Get us out of here."

She looked over the control panel, familiarising herself with the commands. She had just gotten her twelfth hoop when she had last flown a craft with similar controls to this one. Half its touch-screen was shattered. If she could steer that broken piece of junk, she could steer anything.

"Resa, don't you hate flying?"

"Thanks for reminding me, Benjamín."

The mediship awoke, dashboard activating. Resa's stomach flipped, and behind her, Benjamín cursed. They were staring at a guard pointing his weapon directly at the window.

"Recruits, you are not authorised to enter this building." His voice was muffled through the glass. "You are not authorised to be aboard this mediship. Come out with your hands up and allow me to escort you back to the Recruit Suite."

Benjamín gesticulated through the window. That was her cue. She typed the command. The ship shot into the sky, crashing through the docking station's glass doors. Metal grinding; screeching, the ship rapidly climbed, pinning Resa to the floor.

Through the roar of the ship, she heard a gurgling sound, like a drain clogged with mud after a flood. Benjamín rolled onto his back, lungs quivering. Everything in the ship had been dislodged, rattling as it gained altitude. A piece of jagged metal was embedding in his chest.

She hooked fingers in the metal grating; heaved her weight across the ship. Blood soaked his shirt. Too much of it, sickeningly warm. A cry formed in her chest, rising, a lump in her throat.

The ReGen Chamber.

He clung to her as she dragged him to his feet; staggered to the chamber in the rear cabin. One foot first. Good. Now the other. She laid him down on the gel. Blood spluttered from his lips.

Don't drown. Please don't drown.

"I'm sorry." Gently, she eased the metal from his flesh and closed the chamber door. Liquid pooled into the chamber. Benjamín's eyes fluttered shut.

Stumbling to the controls at the front of the ship, Resa let out a cry. She wanted to jam her eyes shut; to make it go away. They were no use to her anyway, clouded as they were with tears. She couldn't see anything; didn't need to. She knew what lay ahead. At every point in the horizon, Rejensy was surrounded by the wall, a solid screen projecting images of a tranquil forest, raised around the city to give the illusion of freedom.

But every wall had a gate and all gates could be opened, if you had the key.

The ship jolted forward, gaining speed. A voice sounded: "Activate departure protocol." Resa typed furiously, triggering an ear-splitting beep with every incorrect sequence.

"Come on, come on!"

Yellow lights blinked around the gate, flickered to red. Resa braced for impact, slammed the dashboard.

"Departure protocol activated."

She laughed as the gates juddered open and a sliver of desert appeared, expanding as they slid apart.

Not fast enough. The side of the mediship clipped the opening as Resa drove it forward, sending them spinning into the barren landscape ahead. With the whoosh of thrusters, the ship levelled.

Resa took a breath, then flicked through the commands.

There. She drew up the map; slid her fingers right until they hovered over the eastern plains. That night on the roof, Benjamín had told her the name of the village he came from. Sangelo.

She hit the point on the map. The ship lurched toward the horizon.

An hour in the air, and a red light flashed on the dashboard: the mediship was travelling at half its capacity. Another hour, another red light, this time signalling fuel supplies dropping dangerously below the minimum.

Night fell. Resa adjusted the mediship's altitude. If all systems failed, both they and the ship had to survive the crash. She couldn't let this all be for nothing.

With no water or food aboard the ship, only medical supplies she didn't know how to use and a distress beacon she fixed to her waist, she took a seat against the chamber, hugging her knees. With a clunking lullaby of the broken ship, she waited for whatever came first: sleep, dawn, or the jolt of metal smacking ground.

Alarms blared. Resa shot her eyes open. The ship's voice thundered through the speakers: "Attention operator. Impact in 2 minutes."

Resa stumbled toward the controls, but the ship tipped, voice turning into a whine, and she tumbled into the wrecked interior. Pain sliced through her, blinded her. Then the world exploded, ship ramming ground. She felt it in her bones; threw up her arms as a shield, but something was wrong. Missing.

Resa tried to sit up, but she couldn't hold her weight, slamming onto her back. She was breathless. Losing consciousness. Losing blood. She forced her eyes on the debris. Focus. Something to tie it off. Something to stem the bleeding.

Her remaining fingers trembled as she wound the cord around what was left of her arm. Holding the end between her teeth, she counted – one, two... Her teeth sank into plastic as she pulled the cord taught.

Stumbling from the ship, Resa cradled her arm. She couldn't let it go; couldn't grow a new one. Not here. Regeneration wasn't given to people like her. Too poor, too ragged; her cells were for printing, not treating. She was a daughter of the slums, and a fool to think she could escape.

The village was a dark silhouette against a purple sky – Benjamín's village – but Resa couldn't walk anymore, limbs too heavy, head pounding. She couldn't breathe; turned on the spot to see a trail of blood in the rocks.

Loosening her grip on her injured arm, she let it slip away, blood-stained hands fumbling for the distress beacon. Pain laced her every move as she pointed it at the sky and fired.

She was so tired. The ground came up to meet her, warm sand welcoming her home. She was desert born and in the desert she would die.

Resa woke to pain in her jaw. It was locked, teeth sore from being clamped while she slept. Fire burned under her skin. She reached to brush the sodden hair from her brow, but nothing moved; her hair stayed plastered to her face. She dropped her phantom limb, letting out a relieved breath. Resa had brought Benjamín home.

Nearly. The ship had crash-landed five miles from Benjamín's village. Camila had bribed the man who found Resa in the rocky plain between ship and village; his silence had cost more than a year's food in tech, but if it kept her brother safe, she would have paid more. Resa owed Camila a debt, and while Benjamín slept, she'd spent the last two months paying it.

She tugged on her boots, a difficult feat without her dominant hand to serve her, then left the room that had been Benjamín's. Camila was still awake, slumped behind her computer, fingers tapping wildly.

"Any changes?"

Camila shook her head. "Same as this afternoon, Resa. A week, maybe two, and we'll have the blueprints ready to go."

She had the same eyes as Benjamín, steel against tan skin. Now they were dark and sunken, and pieces of hair had escaped her ponytail. She couldn't have slept a wink, but to Resa she was a fountain of hope. Camila swore she could replicate any piece of tech if she only had a model to go by. Her confidence made it easier to think; easier to block out the noise.

Wires covered the floor like vines. Carefully, Resa picked a path through.

Camila caught her hand. "We'll have Benjamín back, you wait. He got this far. He won't give up. Not mi hermano. Why don't you go see how he's doing?"

The hoverbike hummed. Pain throbbed in her phantom limb. With the moon as her guide, Resa retraced her steps to the mediship. It lay where she had crash-landed, half-buried in the ground, the rest of its shining hulk hidden beneath blankets she'd found on board and a layer of sand. No one came this far out into the desert except by ship – by day the sun would burn you alive and by night it would freeze your toes. From the skies, the mediship would have looked like just another piece of wreckage on the outskirts of the slums, a carcass already picked clean.

She squeezed through the twisted door onto the ship. It was pitch-black, save for a cold blue light radiating from the rear-cabin.

"Benjamín?"

It felt good to say his name. That he couldn't hear her hurt like a thousand cells being extracted at once. Like the ship, he lay exactly where she'd left him: in the ReGen Chamber, kept alive by its fluids, no longer able to regenerate because of what she'd done. A crack ran along the front panel and the seal was dented, locking Benjamín inside. The hole in Benjamín's chest was halfway to healed, a fleshy web beneath a shirt soaked with blood, still as bright as if it was freshly drawn. Two months he had lain here. Two months he had waited, suspended between life and death.

"I'm going to fix this," Resa whispered, forcing herself to look away from the chamber; away from Benjamín. She picked up one of her tools, crouching under the dashboard, and set to work.

Resa would repair the ship, and Camila would get the blue prints. She would fix the ReGen Chamber, Benjamín would open his eyes, and the desert would have medicine the likes of which it hadn't seen since Rejensy raised its wall. They were desert born, forged in the fires of a ruined sun. They knew suffering and they knew pain. The Treated city didn't know what it had coming.

Elva Hills is an English-American writer based in Edinburgh. She holds an MA(Hons) in History from the University of Aberdeen and an MA in Creative Writing from Edinburgh Napier University. In 2017, she was shortlisted by Penguin Random House UK for the WriteNow mentoring scheme.

The Beachcomber Presents

Mark Toner

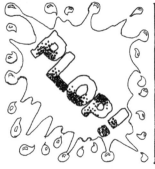

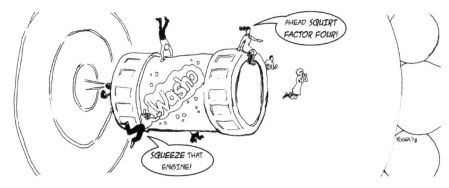

Crossing the Starfield

Or, the philanthropical beauty of second-hand book shops in Glasgow's Merchant City.

Chris Kelso

I was idly strumming the spines of some some well-thumbed vintage science fiction journals in Thistle Books, on Otago street, Glasgow, when my gaze caught sight of a tall, elegant second-hand hardback – *Starfield: Science Fiction by Scottish Writers*.

"I'm having some of this" – I thought-out-loud, and I remember the Thistle Books staff member who was standing nearby me at the time beholding me with contempt over the rim of her trifocals before shuffling off to stand in a different area of the shop. Away from me. So it goes.

I consider myself something of an authority when it comes to Scottish SF. I'm well-versed enough to engage in conversation with anoraks like Hal Duncan and Andrew Wilson, and I even have an alphabetised, Dewey-Decimal-Classified shelf in my own personal library dedicated to all things SF Caledonia – so that gives you some idea of my depth of knowledge.

But I had never heard of *Starfield* before. Hardly anyone had.

Yet it claimed to be the 'first ever anthology of Scottish science fiction'?

How could such a book have dodged my attention for so long?

"Maybe it's terrible and no one wants to acknowledge its existence." – I thought. It wasn't terrible, of course. Even as I held the book in my hand I knew it was special. The pages were tanned, the dust-jacket ragged[1]. It'd certainly seen better days, but it had an eye-catching cover designed by preeminent Dundonian artist

---

1 Interestingly, the book was published in 1989 by The Orkney Press ltd. The company was spearheaded by Howie Firth who now runs the Orkney Science Festival.

Sydney Jordan and a table of contents as impressive as I've seen. The anthology cost 50-bloody-pence.

There was no way I wasn't going to buy it.

In fact, remember the bit in *Raiders of the Lost Arc*, when Indiana Jones reached out for the golden idol in that ancient booby-trapped temple in Peru? – well that was me in Thistle Books; wriggling fingers poised, eyes all agape, ready to retrieve a mysterious artefact from its thrift store boneyard.

I *had* to have it.

The first story, by criminally under-rated and under-published Chris Boyce, really is a barn-storming introduction to proceedings (and I won't spoil it). *The Rig* zooms in on a group of scientists investigating the strange germination of a sea lily on an oil rig platform – a funny, well-written and surprisingly smutty opening gambit. Anyone who has read Boyce's surreal out-of-print novels *Brainfix* and *Catchworld* will know they're in capable hands.

Another attractive thing about the book right off the bat is the presence of renowned writers who don't usually ply their trade in the science fiction field: The mighty Alasdair Gray has two fine little stories here, which he's also beautifully illustrated. *The Crank that Made the Revolution* centres on fictional Cessnock-born inventor, Vague McMenamy, who devises a tandem duck-boat called "the improved duck" which, well…enhances duck mobility. In his second story, the Kafka-esque *The Cause of Recent Change*, Gray throws the reader into the painting department of Glasgow Art School where students must dig their way out of the building and somehow achieve planetary motion.

There is SF poetry from Edwin Morgan, our foremost poet of the 20th century (after reading *Europa* there'll be no reason to ever doubt his credentials in this genre again), and Naomi Mitchison's *What Kind of lesson?* continues the trend. Janice Galloway's *A Continuing Experiment*, an oblique prose poem about an alien race who arrive on earth with unclear intentions and told from the perspective of a detained human observer, is worth a look also.

There is a notable contributions from William King, probably more famous nowadays for his contribution to the *Warhammer* series of novels, and Angus McAllister, a writer I have admired for a long time.[2]

---

2 and whom I have since solicited to write a short story for inclusion in an anthology I edited with Hal Duncan called *Caledonia Dreamin' – Strange Fiction of Scottish Descent* a few years ago.

Starfield also finds a place for the winners and runners-up of Duncan Lunan's fabled Glasgow Herald competition. Richard Hammersley, Elsie W.K. Donald, and Louise Turner – and David John Lee who finished third, but whose story sufficiently impressive Duncan enough to be included anyway – all hold their own with the big guns on show. There is a great vein of humour throughout the stories. David Crooks' tale about a Weegie who meets an alien in a pub is a memorable and hilarious centrepiece, written entirely in the Scots-tongue – full of attitude and quality patter.

Then there's Duncan Lunan's *The Square Fella*, a fascinating science-versus-church story about a group of philosophers who set out on a mission to find out the true shape of their world – situated on a bowl-slope between two mountains.

Starfield is a richly textured masterpiece, and it continues to baffle me to this day. The anthology took Duncan Lunan five years to compile, yet it seems to have evaded the critical outlets of the time and there have been no retrospective shouts for a renaissance of interest in celebration of it's achievements. There was literally no publicity for this book, nothing archived online anyway. Nothing on Goodreads, hardly anything on amazon, or any review websites. I hope this changes when it gets a much deserved reissue. Don't let it dodge your attention like it did mine. For a book with Edwin Morgan in it, this would be simply too unpoetic. I hope all the important people grab this golden idol and praise it as an important relic of the nation's science fiction canon – *the first anthology of Scottish science fiction*. Then you'll see what I was so excited about Mrs-Thistle-Books-staff-member, you'll see….

Chris Kelso is an award-winning genre writer, editor, and illustrator from Scotland. His short stories and articles have appeared in publications across the UK, US, and Canada, including SF Signal, Daily Science Fiction, Dark Discoveries, Sensitive Skin, Antipodean-SF, The Airgonaut, Verbicide and many more.

Starfield - science fiction by Scottish writers, edited by Duncan Lunan, is republished by Shoreline of Infinity in June 2018.

£11.95, 240pages, available in paperback from
www.shorelineofinfinity.com
and all good bookshops.

The Square Fella

Duncan Lunan

from *Starfield*

"The Duke has withdrawn his support for your project."
The visitor was having difficulty with the thin air at this altitude, having flown straight up from the coast with no time for acclimatisation. In the briefing room, he was outnumbered by Leon, Michael, Gordon and Beatrice; but if either factor reduced his assurance, he did not allow it to show. "You are to suspend operations at once, and return with me to the city."

"Out of the question!" Leon snapped. "We are in the final stages of preparation. I could argue that it would be more dangerous now to dismantle the rocket than to launch. *Certainly* it would be more dangerous to leave it upright. That vehicle out there is the most powerful ever assembled by man! "

"Just the point, sir," said the Duke's envoy. "His Highness's neighbours have grown concerned. From this high ground, your vehicle could deliver a ton or more of explosives or incendiaries to any city around the central sea. You and the Duke must prove that your intention is purely scientific, before you may proceed."

"The point is absurd," said Michael. "I speak as calculator of the trajectory. To reach any lowland point from here, the rocket would have to rise thousands of miles, as indeed it is intended to do. But the same could be achieved with a smaller vehicle from anywhere downslope, and with more accuracy."

"I am not an expert in these matters," said the envoy, brushing the objection aside. "They will be for the Church to decide, when the objectors' petitions are heard."

"As I thought," said Leon. "The Church is the principal objector, is it not?"

"Your ideas are well known to be controversial. Personally, I take no interest in academic disputes…"

"And yet you are here to intervene in one, and in the most drastic fashion! Let me show you what is at stake." Leon crossed to the first of the charts on the wall. "Here is our world, as we perceive it: a great bowl, with the life-giving sea at its centre. As we travel away from the sea, the slope grows ever steeper and the air more thin – as you notice." The visitor had subsided into a chair and was visibly short of breath. "We are only twenty-five miles upslope. Ten miles from here, you could not remain conscious without breathing apparatus. Seven hundred and fifty miles up, we now know, the atmosphere becomes negligible and there is no vestige of life. By long tradition, the four great mountains on the ridges above us are the comers by which the Gods hold up the world, like a great sheet.

"If they released their hold, the sheet would flatten, the air and water spread out, and life would be extinguished. But can we believe that — *how* can we believe it — when we learn that the ridges are four thousand miles above us; the mountains seventeen hundred and fifty miles higher still; so that most of the Bowl is barren and lifeless."

"What alternative is there? Are you an atheist, sir, do you argue that the existence of life in these favoured conditions is an accident?"

"No, no, that's too absurd to consider. But what we *must* consider is that the world is not shaped as we see it. Are you familiar with the results of Colom's expedition?"

"A vast effort, which the Queen herself had to finance, at great cost and to no purpose. A madman, driven by some supposed insight about a world beyond the Bowl, travelled thousands of miles through airless waste. He failed to reach the ridge, and only that saved him from plunging off into the infinity beyond."

"That's the official version," said Leon. "What wasn't given out, and very few of us know, is that when the slope grew too steep near the top, Colom left the vehicle and went up alone, with breathing apparatus. He reached the ridge, stood upon it, and saw what lay beyond."

"And that was?" Not even this visitor could refrain from asking, though he feigned indifference.

"Another Bowl – from that high viewpoint, indistinguishable from our own. A descending slope, at right-angles to the one he had climbed, and extending equally far below him."

"Probably it *was* our own. Your madman was too far gone from weakness and lack of air to tell the difference, I suppose."

"I have another suggestion," said Leon, turning to the next diagram. "Ever since we've had aircraft – and with everyone living on a slope, *that* was inevitable – men have been trying to use them for warfare, to drop things from them and shoot things at them. We wouldn't have rockets otherwise. But once projective theory was perfected – for which we have Michael here to thank – it was discovered that the centre of attraction in our world lies four thousand miles below the centre of the Bowl."

"And so?"

"And so that allows a much vaster world than we supposed. If the North ridge has another Bowl beyond it, the same must be true of the other ridges – and the far ridges of those Bowls – and so on, around the surface of a spheroid. Each Bowl could have its own air, ocean and life … even intelligent life, though completely isolated from our own."

"And each with its own Gods, at its comers, living on those airless plateaux you've drawn between the mountains? I see now why you have to be stopped. Even the speculation is dangerous, and I shall report as much. In giving foundations to the Bowl, you remove support from the faith! For the record, how many worlds and Gods do you postulate?"

"Thirty-six Bowls, at the least, though one must be smaller than our own. As for Gods, who can say?"

"You have already said quite enough!" A fit of coughing racked the envoy, as he rose to his feet. "By the authority of the Church and the Duke, I order you to cease all preparations, and dismantle what is in hand … "

"No," said Leon. The sheer effrontery of it took the envoy's breath away, and in this high place, he would have trouble regaining it. As he collapsed, coughing violently, he managed to gasp. "The troops will stop you …"

"As I thought," said Michael, pushing the others towards the door. "Those rumours of manoeuvres in the highlands were just too convenient. Leon, we must launch at once. Gordon, are you ready?"

"You can't just leave that man in there – " Beatrice protested. But the two philosophers had already gone, one to the control room and the other towards the rocket.

"He's less danger to us immobilised in there." Gordon told her. "No doubt someone will get him an air cylinder … I have to get ready for the flight. And I have to make sure Leon and Michael get you out of here, on one of the aircraft, before the troops arrive." Beatrice was the only woman here, as a special privilege to himself, and he didn't want her to fall into the hands of the Duke's enemies.

"We should have had more time!" They had followed Leon, more slowly, towards the rocket which now towered ahead of them. "Gordon, it's so dangerous. Is it worth it, just to learn the shape of the world?"

"It's time to find out – it's as simple as that. Don't worry, I'll come back." He kissed her in the midst of the activity Leon had galvanised, and left her to climb the gantry which would soon be wheeled away.

"Let's go over it once again," said Leon, as Gordon settled himself in the couch. "Your launch will be vertical, all the way. Peak altitude will be sixty thousand miles, fifteen world radii, flight time will be twenty-four hours. Centripetal attraction will be enough to make sure you come down in air. You'll be high enough at peak to see clearly into the surrounding Bowls. And if that other crazy idea is correct, and the world rotates under you, you'll travel in effect along a great circle, over ten of the Bowls in all, and land at a symmetrical point on the far side of our own – in which case Colom's crew will pick you up. Better hope that's true, if there are troops on the way here," he added, brusquely, and clasped Gordon's hand before banging shut the hatch.

Now there was time to think about it, in the long pause before the launch. Time to think about the failure of the previous test, the attempt to put a reflecting sphere like an artificial sun into orbit around the world. The trajectory had been good, according to observers upslope, but the speck had never reappeared over the rim of the world, though the observers remained on station until lack of air forced them down. Hence the plan, this time, to go straight up and remain in view throughout – unless of course the world really did rotate with respect to the stars and the sun …

How could appearances be so deceptive? Impressed as he was by Colom's account, if only in defiance of the clerical critics, what kind of Gods could create so misleading a world? The team had discussed this only the previous night, over a bottle of wine, thinking they still had days to prepare for the mission. Had they all met before, Leon had speculated, in another Bowl or even another world, and argued over its shape – perhaps a very different shape from this? Michael had pointed out the regularities of the world: the stars, for instance, evenly spaced and giving just enough warmth to keep the Bowl from freezing at night. "Perhaps it's not a true cosmos – just a bubble, or a box. A great All-Fool's 'joke' by the Gods, or beings less than gods."

The lowlands were abuzz with the issue, from the coastal cities to the highest towns on the periphery. The argument wasn't just between science and the church: the patrons of the rocket and crawler programmes had their own rivalries, and duels had been fought over the merits of two approaches which should have been complementary. Only the faithful could accept that the issue shouldn't be settled by experiment, and the supposed military threat of Leon's rocket was pure invention. Anyone who believed that would believe that the grazing herds up here had longer legs on one side that the other, to run at high speed around the slope of the Bowl.

These were stupendous days, Gordon and Beatrice had agreed, as they had watched the descending sun reflected on the burnished flank of the rocket. When it was gone, the glare of the work lights had almost obliterated the even spread of stars glowing above them. "If faith rests on a lie," they had pledged later, "let faith fall!" The challenge and the daring of their response made it seem as if nothing could stop them; but the envoy from downslope had returned them to reality. It had taken all the power of Colom's patrons, including the Queen, to keep him out of prison or the insane asylum. If troops overran the launch site, destroying the rocket or arresting the scientists, Leon's patron could do little about it. It was not an issue over which to go to war.

Outside, the aircraft had taken off to sweep the surrounding slope before the launch. Gordon had insisted Beatrice be in one, to escape if there were soldiers closing in. And sure enough, one of the aircraft was back already, warning lights flashing to the periscopes of the armoured control room.

If only they could exchange spoken messages! Some of the experimenters in the Duke's laboratories believed they could make it possible, across the central sea or even to the heights Gordon would reach today. Objectors had wanted the mission postponed until that would be possible. But as he had told Beatrice, it was time to find the answer *now*. As if to confirm it, a red flare soared from the blockhouse, and beneath him brilliant flame cracked into being at the base of the rocket. The Launch Master gave the solid-fuel thrust a moment to stabilise before releasing the clamps, and then he was away, watching the shadow of the rocket and the smoke trail racing the vehicle itself up-slope. His fate would be governed by the gyroscopes in Leon's steering system: he had no control, and in any case the acceleration held him immobile as expected.

Going up vertically, with reference to gravity, he was out of the air much faster than he would have been climbing or flying up the slope. There was a little buffeting at first, but that soon faded away. Already the grasslands were thinning out, well away to port; patterns of moss and lichen, with no snow at this time of year, merged into bare rock. He was out of the atmosphere: he saw sunlight flash on the lens of one of Leon's high-altitude trackers. The heliograph messages had alerted at least one team in time for them to cover the early launch.

The first stage burned out, plunging him into the weightlessness he had sometimes generated in soaring aircraft. He counted off the seconds, one, two, three, *four,* and the second stage fired and disconnected. A brief oscillation, caught by the gyros and the vanes, and up, up he went, the jet roaring closer behind him now, while outside the sky turned black and the stars came out, as he had seen them in sunlight when training up-slope. The acceleration wasn't unbearable; higher than in the water-driven centrifuge, but more purposeful, with the knowledge that he was actually going somewhere. The gyros showed no deviation from the vertical climb, the graphite vanes in the exhaust had not been needed. The face of the Bowl, off to port, was a racing blur of light and shadow, still constantly receding. Only the failed satellite had gone higher than this.

The capsule tumbled as the charge sputtered out and expelled him, but the cold gas jets let him stabilise it. With the heat shield pointed towards the sun, and the Bowl inverted "above" him, he seemed to be falling out of it into space. But in fact he was slowing constantly, as the central mass pulled him back. The entry shield was facing the sun, out of sight below, so it shouldn't be necessary to rotate the capsule to cool it. There was a periscope arrangement with a revolving mirror, so that he could continue observations even if spinning proved necessary, but it would limit his field of view. For the moment, the shield seemed to be coping.

He was amazed at how much he could see from this altitude. For a while, even without the telescope the patterns of cultivated land were clear in the lowland plains. The overall circulation of the clouds was clearly displayed, and below them he could see concentric rings of colour in the central sea. He was noting down all observations, just in case he shouldn't be alive when the capsule returned to the Bowl, though of all possibilities that seemed the least likely, when life-support systems had been so thoroughly developed in the slope crawler programme. The cost had been high, recorded in the notebooks of failed expeditions – the notebooks of men who would walk away from a failed crawler, to give their companions more time to wait for rescue. If his own life was to be forfeited, well, others had gone that way before. Better to die seeking answers than at the hands of the Church which forbade the questions.

Within an hour, he had confirmed the less likely hypothesis under test. The Bowl *was* rotating, leaving him behind as he rose out of it; his vertical climb was taking on the elliptic contour of a ballistic trajectory. The observers below would see him moving westward among the stars, falling behind the creeping sun, if they still had him. Inevitably, now, he must go over the rim of the world like the failed satellite, and he had only Michael's word that inevitably he must return. If the world was not symmetrical, he was doomed – but there was more exhilaration in it than fear.

By the second hour, however, the spheroidal hypothesis was in trouble. He should by now have been over the western edge of the Bowl, had Leon been right, but instead he had still to pass over the central sea. If he had been deflected back towards the east ridge from the vertical during the second-stage burn, he would now be crossing the Bowl too slowly, higher than he should be, and would come down in some other bowl on the great circle or on one of the airless plateaux between them. That at least would be a quick death, since only air could slow the capsule down. In another Bowl, there might be a higher civilisation which could help him get home …

But the gyros had been true, according to the instruments. If so, the geometry of the world had to be quite different from Leon's prediction. Since the Bowl turned under sun and stars, and the central mass lay far below it, was there a counterweight beyond that? He would be at his furthest from the centre when he passed it; but if was less massive and further from the centre than the Bowl, collision might be inevitable. It would explain the disappearance of the satellite. What an extraordinary way to die, smeared flat like an insect, amid the ruins of drawings no-one would ever see.

The known world had shrunk to a misty, distorted patch in the centre of the rocky expanse of the Bowl. The face below him swept evenly round to encompass it, the effect of its concavity much less than he had expected. Perhaps his eyes were over-compensating for the lack of atmospheric refraction. The sun had passed over the western edge, still drawing ahead of him, and was illuminating whatever lay beyond. Soon Gordon, too, would be able to see over the approaching ridge. He forced himself to down some food, and waited in suspense as the world turned slowly below.

He could see over the ridge now, and there was another slope beyond. Far beyond, there lay another ridge, broken in places by steep slides of rock. There was a world outside the Bowl, and it was another Bowl, edged with ridges and mountains of its own —

But with straight edges. There were no high-altitude, airless plateaux, inhabited by Gods or otherwise. The two 'Bowls' met at the West ridge, all the way along, and now that he was over it he could see that the ridge itself was a straight line. The new 'Bowl's' inner face dropped steeply away from it, at an exact right-angle to the old, and from this height neither face showed any concavity whatever. At last he could dismiss the distortions of perspective, compensate for the vastness of the view, and recognise what he truly saw. The shock was overwhelming.

"The World is a cube!" Gordon wrote on his pad, and he underlined till he couldn't draw for laughing and the capsule was rocking. The wildest theorist patronised by the Duke would never have dreamed of it. All down the ages the priests had likened the Bowl to a great square of cloth, held up by the Gods at its four corners to keep the air and water in the centre. And behold, gravity alone was responsible, the square had been flat all along – not just flat, not just a square, but the face of a *cube*! Laughter threatened to overwhelm him again. He could see, now, that the second face had its own central pool of air and water – and perhaps living beings, fooled by their Gods into thinking they lived in a Bowl which was the whole of Creation.

To his trained eye, it was obvious that it had been created. In vacuum the mountains were very bright, like cut gems. *Cut gems, deliberately shaped.* Though half-obscured by rock slides, there were faint lines of stress emanating from them, diagonals and intersecting curves, as if space itself was distorted to hold the world in shape. Surely only Gods could make a world, much less keep it in a shape which was against its raw nature. Could it all just be to create niches for life, as if for study? The true purpose was unfathomable.

Somehow he must get back to reveal this, whatever the personal cost. He had been sketching assiduously; they wouldn't put this down to lack of oxygen, or heat exhaustion. But was return possible? Obviously the Gods' web of forces must affect his trajectory, and if he got outside it, he might never come down but drift forever amid the lattice of stars.

The face below held a world larger than his own, so the air must be thicker. Certainly the clouds were higher and more extensive, giving only glimpses of the surface below. The central sea was much bigger down there, and temperatures were obviously higher. He saw no sign of intelligence, though from this height, that proved little. If there was life down there on the second face, it might be quite unlike his own; the two 'Bowls' were as completely isolated as if they sat on different worlds. The towering barrier of the ridge had to be overcome for any kind of contact, and only intelligent life could make that effort. No birds, insects or winds crossed the ridge to seed one place with the life of the other, and thousands of miles of rock separated them underground. Would it be possible to make a tunnel through? A vehicle could "fall" through it, slowing after the midpoint. Beyond doubt, knowing that other 'Bowls' existed, men like Leon and Colom would want to visit them.

His own Bowl was lost to view. On the assumption that he would have stayed over it, he had been scheduled to sleep for six hours during the flight; and as he gained height and the view became less detailed, he allowed sleep to take him. When he awoke, he was over the third face of the cube, and beginning to descend. Michael's predictions might yet bring him home, though certainly not where troops directed by the Church would be expecting him. What else, he wondered, was happening behind him meantime? Had Beatrice made good her escape, and were Leon and Michael now facing the wrath of the Church? Or had they tracked the capsule, guessing wrongly from his slow movement west, and given him up for lost? Even so, some members of the team would be envying him what he must he seeing now, impossible though it would be for them to imagine: from this height, he could see the world plainly as a cube.

The third face was much different at the centre, with thin air, no sea, and hardly any clouds. Markings under the cap of atmosphere suggested there might once have been a sea, but if so the water had long since escaped. Bands of red and ochre stained the ground, as though the surface had oxidised. Gordon could see no clear signs of life, though some circular forms might be the work of intelligence; like the traces of some colossal bombardment.

The capsule was well on its way down, beginning to overtake the sun as it gained speed on the descending leg of its trajectory. By now Gordon was sure the trajectory itself was correct: he would come down at sunrise on the western edge of the known Bowl. He would be glad to have the sun back under the shield, meantime – he had had to spin the capsule several times to cool it, using up precious gas, and the glare was an annoyance.

The fourth face, as he crossed it, was another extreme: a turbulent, opaque atmosphere, streaked with colours and sometimes lit from below by the flashes of violent storms.

Were these the laboratories where the Gods tried out their ideas, on the formation of life and its evolution? It had been suggested, though with great caution, that life in his own Bowl had not always been as it was today: it was a matter on which the Church had yet to rule. The differing conditions on the four faces might represent different stages in the evolution of life, or perhaps evolution in different conditions. The polar faces must be dead, in permanent shadow except where ridges caught the sun, unless the warmth from the stars was enough to keep the air gaseous and sustain something strange in the twilight.

His mission should be repeated in darkness, to look for city lights on the other faces ...

Well ahead of the sun, Gordon passed over the last ridge into his own 'Bowl', a vast black field cutting off the stars. He was right on schedule: the trackers should pick him up easily, since he was in full sunlight. As he hurtled on, he had to hope for the last required accuracy: it would be tragic to miss the atmosphere and end the mission by crashing on to bare rock. As he turned the capsule for the final descent, above him he saw a great cascade of light down the ridges as the Sun broke over the edge of the Bowl.

He had set the vehicle spinning, and a fiery glow built up around it as he plunged towards the western slope. This, he realised, was the Gods' last chance: he was coming back with the shape of the world, the plurality of worlds, and doubts of the Gods' godhood. It was the last chance to bum him with his knowledge.

The chance was missed. The fire died away, the capsule's fins were extended to stop the spin. The parachutes opened and the falling craft steadied in the sky, over the forests of the west highlands. Down there, Colom would be organising aircraft and ground parties to search for him. They must plan how to spread the new knowledge: slowly, by secret organisation, or shouted from the housetops at risk of martyrdom?

He hoped there would be time to decide. One way or another, his knowledge *must* be spread. His mind lingered on that as the capsule descended into the trees, marching like an army down the long slope of the land.

Duncan Lunan has been a full time author, researcher, lecturer, broadcaster, editor, critic and tutor since 1970, specialising in astronomy, spaceflight and science fiction. He has published 9 books, 38 short stories and nearly 1500 articles. *The Elements of Time*, a collection of Duncan's time travelling short stories was published by *Shoreline of Infinity*.

Moon
Flash Fiction Competition for
Shoreline of Infinity Readers

Fifty years ago, in December 1968, three astronauts circled the Moon for the first time. In this, our second annual flash fiction competition, we are looking for flash fiction science fiction stories on the the theme of the Moon. It could be any moon in time or space, and it's up to you who, or what we meet.

We're looking for flash fiction, which we're defining as a maximum of 1,000 words.

Just remember, *Shoreline of Infinity* is a science fiction(ish) magazine, and your story must be science-fictional.

Prizes:

£40 for the winning story plus 1 year digital subscription to *Shoreline of Infinity*. Two runners-up will receive 1 year digital subscription to Shoreline of Infinity.

The top three stories will be published in *Shoreline of Infinity* – All three finalists will receive a print copy of this edition.

Also

The best stories submitted (up to a maximum of 20,000 words in total) will be published in 2019 in an anthology, and each contributor will receive a digital copy and a pro-rata share of the royalties.

The Detail

Maximum 1,000 words.

Maximum 2 stories per submitter.

Deadline for entries: midnight (UK time) 30th September 2018.

To enter, visit the website at:
www.shorelineofinfinity.com/2018ffc

There's no entry fee, but on the submission entry form you will be asked for a secret code word only obtainable from reading issue 12 of *Shoreline of Infinity*, hence: competition for Shoreline of Infinity Readers.

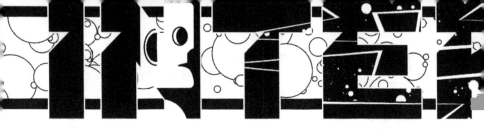

Interview: Ada Palmer

Eris Young asks the questions

Eris Young: *An interesting question with far-future sci fi is whether current circumstances might make the fictional world in question possible – how do you think the social structure in* Terra Ignota *might come about in 400 years, from today's sociopolitical climate?*

Ada Palmer: One example I've been thinking about recently is one of the ones that's least visible in the book. I wish I could explore it in more depth because I think it's an important idea – it's that this culture has had a revolution in what is enviable, what you think of as being the mark of someone who's super successful. It isn't wealth or political power: the core of that being that when you move into automation enough, the number of hours people have to work to keep civilisation running drops.

In renaissance Florence the work week was three days. Because wages were really high

the value of labour was really high – this was also related to the Black Death: when you have a sudden labour shortage, wages go up. So believe it or not, in Renaissance Florence people genuinely did just work three days a week and spend the rest of the time hanging around talking about art – I'm not kidding, we have documentation about this.

In this civilisation that's the case. People start valuing their time and liberty more, at which point envying or admiring somebody for being rich starts to weaken as a cultural value. And so there is in this future a kind of admiration for people who are a *vocateur*, who love their work and choose to put in extra hours, but when you look at a celebrity magazine, it's not how much wealth they've managed to accumulate, it's how much fun they manage to have with the time they have – whether it's a spectacular party

Ada Palmer is an historian, an author of science fiction and fantasy, and a composer. She teaches in the History Department at the University of Chicago. Her latest books, *Seven Surrenders* and *The Will to Battle* of the acclaimed Terra Ignota series are reviewed on page 116.

or a really impressive trip to go on, or just someone who really ostentatiously has fun, in visible ways – that's the celebrity culture of this civilisation. And there's no reason things couldn't change like that.

The way we decide who should be envied or admired shifts historically. In medieval times what you admire in a woman – piety, how much time she spends interacting with the church – is not what our celebrity magazines admire about women. When I talk to people who comment on *XYZ* attribute of a positive future, whether it's Terra Ignota or another, being implausible, they'll often cite, *human nature is X* – often with a component of, *people will always selfishly want to get rich*. And the answer is, so long as getting rich is an enviable state, some people will. There will still be people who will work really hard to get what's enviable,

but what's enviable will not necessarily always be the same.

EY: *I'm also interested in the way gender is handled in the story. Can you talk a bit about what you wanted to explore with genderplay, and where the system in the books comes from?*

AP: There's a couple different elements I'm intending to explore in the gender play. One of them is about the reader's experience seeing the pronouns flow while knowing they don't match what we would do as cis assignment in standard society at the present, and the other is the social comment element of it.

The experiential aspect of this is to make people hyper distrustful of pronouns. You'll have a person that's consistently had one pronoun then there'll be a moment of whiplash. And I've been delighted by how it makes a lot of readers rethink how the gender tag they associated with a character made them feel differently about that character. One of my techniques working on the book was, two-thirds of the way through the outline, I went through and asked myself, how different does it feel if each character one by one were assigned the other gender? Does this character's story arc suddenly feel like a particular archetype, or suddenly not feel like an archetype? Does it suddenly feel as if a romance ought to develop between character A and character B? And I made some shifts at that point in which pronouns I had Mycroft use.

Then there's Mycroft's claim that gender still haunts this future, even though for 200 years this future has only used the neutral "they" pronoun. I want the reader to be thinking critically about that claim, and the different characters who articulate different versions of that. We hear different variants on the idea that the gender binary isn't inescapable or biologically ingrained, but it's so deep in human culture that this civilisation did not succeed in rooting out unspoken and often unconscious assumptions about gender.

A phrase I've used in a couple recent conversations is "deep nurture"; people ask *is it nature or nurture?*, well, it's a level of nurture that neither the nurturer or the nurturee is conscious even happened, but

absolutely *is* a learned thing.

There's a great study of interactions between people and one-day-olds: the instant a child is born, the first interaction an adult can have on a physical level is to put out your finger, and the baby will grip it. And at least within American society, if the adult interacting with the infant perceives the infant as male, they'll tug, to test the strength of the infant. And if we perceive the infant to be female we won't. So we're already treating the infant very slightly differently. We don't know, yet, how our unintended nurturing affects kids based on our perceptions of them.

So this future had the Church War, this cataclysmic world war. In the aftershock, because on both sides the most ferocious combatants were also the ones that had the most traditional gender roles, gender-*ing* got associated with the worst side of humanity. Everyone said, *okay, we've lost gender and we'll never talk about it again*, and never looked deeply at those tiny, inadvertent and unconscious elements of nurture that hadn't been rooted out. Like how after the Civil War in the US everyone just declared racial equality was there. And that's why race relations were able to persist and be so bad, because society is lying to itself about this problem. I wanted to portray a society that has stopped working on gender and declared a false victory.

EY: *Terra Ignota draws lots of influence from classical sources that the average reader might not be conversant with. Does it feel like a leap of faith to put your work out there and trust people will still connect with it?*

AP: I always imagine multiple readers as I'm working on a chapter. I think, what will this feel like to a reader who is a classicist, who will get every classical allusion, as opposed to a reader who's a major science fiction fan, or a reader who's reading it for the second time? I'll try to make sure that if this paragraph is supposed to be an emotional climax, there's something in it to be an emotional climax whether or not you get the classical allusion. Yesterday I wrote a sentence thinking, wow, the people who have recently read *The Odyssey* will totally recognise this particular simile to a rock, everyone else won't. But it doesn't harm or aid your understanding of what's happening as a whole or even of the characters; it's an easter egg.

EY: *And how does it feel to have received what seems like an overwhelmingly positive response?*

AP: I never expected it to have as big a readership as it's had, and neither did Tor. It's a *really* hard book. So we always expected it to find an enthusiastic but niche audience. So to have it be a Hugo finalist and get as much discussion as it did was unexpected and incredible and made me very happy. Because what I most want is for ppl to engage with the ideas. I feel as a writer that I've received amazing great works that gave me ideas from people earlier in the grand conversation of science fiction, and I felt I wanted to reply to that and and give other people new ideas. My ideal is that people then respond to that with their own ideas and carry on the conversation.

EY: *How does being a historian interact with your work as a writer of science fiction?*

AP: The main thing it does is affect my worldbuilding and the palette of questions I want to ask of a society. It trains me to think a lot about details of culture, of economics, that I think a lot of people come to unquestioned. If I'm thinking about the development of Terra Ignota and I'm thinking alright, there's another world war. In the world war, like the last one, we lose lots of really good art, because when major cities get bombed, major cities have art museums. But with advances in 3D printing, what is a civilisation's response to the destruction of a famous piece of art? They build a replica. How is that going to affect the way people value replica vs original? How is that going to affect the art market? How is that going to affect new movements in art?

And it's from working through all those interconnections – we don't ever hear about those art movements, but we do occasionally hear about other bits of tech that I realised they would have to have, if they made the tech 100 years earlier to recreate the lost art. So they have to have computer printing that can reproduce marble effectively – so that's going to affect the way they're building buildings. All of that is semi-invisible, but that's what makes me come up with an original idea for the cityscape. People keep saying, *you have so many ideas*, but rather than having 1000 different ideas, these are all just integrated nodes on a thoroughly worked-through world. But the core of that is you have to be okay with it being ninety-percent invisible. You're showing a tip of the iceberg.

EY: *Would you consider writing historical fiction?*

AP: Yes, the next series I'm doing is vikings, though mostly Viking myths, so we're gonna see more of gods than we do of people. And I will eventually do an Italian renaissance fiction piece, but because I learn more about the Italian renaissance every day, if I wait another decade it'll be better than if I write it now. But I find historical fiction more difficult in some ways. Mostly the renaissance is intimidating because all my colleagues will judge it.

I'm actually very relaxed about the historical detail question – everyone expects me to be persnickety about, is *X* accurate, and I'll say I don't care how accurate it is, because I see how often we are wrong. So even if you wrote the most perfectly researched possible historical fiction book, a few years later we would discover a new thing. So while I respect good research, to me the important thing is, did you use the historical material available to you to make a great story?

There was a life-changing moment for me when I was doing my PhD, and I was sitting with some friends on our livingroom floor watching *Buffy the Vampire Slayer*, and it was the episode with Anya's backstory – we see her as a medieval German peasant, she's surrounded by bunnies, and these domesticated bunnies are breeding and it's part of the ongoing *Anya's afraid of bunnies* joke. I released this long sigh, and my friend said, *what's wrong?* And I said, *she's not of a sufficiently high social status to have domesticated rabbits that far north in Europe in that century.* But I only knew that because I went to a presentation where the not-yet-published research that proves this to be true was circulated by a grad student who only figured it out last month. There was literally no way they could have gotten it right. The knowledge wasn't available.

And that is true of history all the time. Writing historical fiction can't be about being accurate – we have to make it about this amazing palette of information that we have about the past – did you use it to do something powerful? And so ever since then I've never criticised a work of fiction for being wrong about a thing, only for making a bad narrative choice.

EY: *What else is on the horizon for you?*

AP: After the Viking mythology series, I'm working on a couple of other things. Probably after that will be a very dark survival horror thing, but I've also got a lighter, almost comedy standalone novel planned out. I wanted to do that sequence anyway but writer friends advised me that it's ideal for your first couple of series to be very different from each other, because that scopes out a lot of space in which people expect you to work. So I think *Terra Ignota*, Viking mythology and survival horror will map out a nice triangle in which I can do all sorts of things. But they will all have metaphysics.

I'm also doing nonfiction projects. Cory Doctorow and I, along with another historian called Adrian Johns, are doing a project on the history of censorship. The goal is to look at how innovations in information technology stimulate new forms of censorship and information control. We're in the middle of that right now with the digital revolution, but the printing press caused a similar sequence of both innovative technology and innovations in how censorship efforts were shaped. Every week over the course of the fall, we're going to fly a pair of experts in, one who works on digital and one who works on printing press, to talk about a particular topic and film it, put it online so it's available to everyone, and to make a public conversation about this.

A lot of academic research is very exciting but it takes three or four years for it to come out, because as it should be academia is very careful and likes to cite everything a hundred times. But the online videos will be a way to share cutting edge research right away, and let everybody who's interested in the question have access to it. So that's my exciting nonfiction.

find out more about Ada Palmer at www.adapalmer.com

Eris Young is a writer of speculative fiction who moved from Southern California to Edinburgh for the lit scene and, apparently, the damp. They've reviewed for *Shoreline of Infinity*, *ScotsGay*, the *Fountain* and *Copperfield Review*. Their fiction has appeared in *Bewildering Stories*, *Esoterica*, *Scrutiny Journal* and *F, M or Other: Quarrels with the Gender Binary*. They tweet at @young_e_h

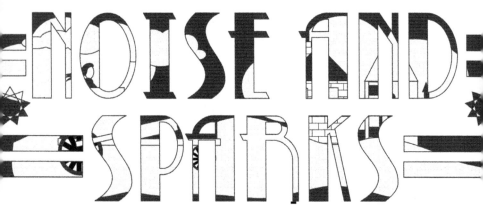

Who's Afraid of the Big Bad Genre?

Ruth EJ Booth

Margaret Atwood, winner of the Arthur C. Clarke Award, dismissed science fiction as "talking squids in outer space." Kazuo Ishiguro, on releasing a novel with an Arthurian setting and a dragon, became concerned his readers might be "prejudiced against surface elements" of *The Buried Giant*.[1] While some such as Helen Sedgwick "enjoy leaving things up to the reader to decide", many writers of what we call SF or fantasy worry when their works are called anything other than Literary Fiction.[2]

Ishiguro's fear of prejudice isn't without foundation: even in their recent obituary for pivotal SF publisher Livia Gollancz, industry magazine *The Bookseller* disparaged the genre.[3] Damien Walter's argument against Atwood's *The Handmaid's Tale* being "pigeon holed" [sic] as SF features three points often trotted out against genre: firstly, the question of quality; secondly, the risk of inappropriate marketing; and thirdly, the impact of novels marketed as SF rather than general fiction.[4]

Regarding quality, Walter declares: "[*The Handmaid's Tale's*] literary lineage is closer to *The Collector* by John Fowles than anything by Arthur C Clarke." Certainly, no one is saying Atwood's novel is like Clarke's work, but neither can the genre of 1985 – or indeed, today – be characterized by the works of one golden-age writer of science utopias. Philip K. Dick had already explored cultural authenticity under colonization in 1962's *Man in the High Castle*, the same year Anthony Burgess tackled the computational theory of the mind in the ultraviolent *A Clockwork Orange*; meanwhile 1985 also saw the release of Ursula K. Le Guin's *Always Coming Home* and David Brin's *The Postman* – one a combination of fictional ethnographic record and autobiography, one a more straight-forward post-apocalyptic novel. All were regarded as SF by critics of the time.

Perhaps Walter's argument is about writing style. "SFF is often thought of as not very well written (despite our absolutely stunning prose stylists like Aliette de Bodard, Catherynne Valente, etc)," notes bookseller D Franklin, "and a literary author renowned for style doesn't want to be associated with that." Even for the '80s, this argument seems ill-conceived: we might note, for example, the sharply-observed prose of Ursula K. Le Guin's (1972) *The World for World is Forest*.

Notably, there are differences between the prose of literary fiction and SF. Publisher David Thomas Moore explains, "some writers may see the division, not in the presence or absence of tropes... but in the importance placed on plot. Not that they see their work as inferior to genre, but different, in that genre invariably regards plot as crucial." A difference in kind, then. Even so, with writers like Jeff Noon following Dick's lead and pushing the metafictional envelope, SF cannot be pinned down to a specific style.

Walter's next point is easier to tackle: "Imagine an alternate timeline where *The Handmaid's Tale* was published as science fiction. Possibly in the kind of pulp cover that many novels featuring women enslaved to strange obsessive Nazis often featured, with a subtitle [*sic*] like 'I was a captive of fundamentalist perverts!', and shipped out to bookshops, as one of many sci-fi novels released in

1985." This seems unlikely: the original cover of Douglas Adams's (1987) *Dirk Gently's Holistic Detective Agency* simply depicted a nameplate in a ray of light. While Lois McMaster Bujold's '80s covers featured women in slinky slit dresses, this is far from the erotic extremes described by Walter.

Walter may have a point regarding the impact of novels marketed as SF. Moore states: "the emotional impact, subtlety of characterisation and subtextual elegance on show in the best genre fiction meets and exceeds even the most pretentious commentator's standards for literary fiction." However, he admits: "Frankly, we in our profession will follow the money: if we think we've got a shot at Richard and Judy's Book Club and your local weekly reading group, we'll slap a moody black and white photo on your book and call it 'fiction,' even as we fume at the distinction." Ultimately, publishing is a business – and authors need to eat. As Moore notes, "the Atwoods and Ishiguros may have jumped, or may have been pushed."

However, Walter's argument isn't about size, but the kind of the impact *The Handmaid's Tale* would have had as SF. Comparing the hypothetical SF …*Tale* with other works, he states: "The men who founded Gilead probably read and enjoyed John Norman's *Gor* novels. And enjoyed their fantasy so much, they used murder and violence to enforce it as America's new reality." Walter argues simply labelling *The Handmaid's Tale* as SF would have changed its interpretation, and by whom. "If we're going to understand, and change for the better, our reality, we need to clearly recognise the work of writers, artists and other creators, who are doing more than selling us escapist fantasies."

The assumptions implicit in these remarks require some unpacking: that SF is a) purely escapist fantasy, and b) as fantasy, it can only be dangerous. Apart from the little self-restraint and inability to distinguish fantasy from reality Walter assigns to his gender, we could ask several questions at this point. Is Pratchett's *Unseen Academicals* incapable of insights into class relationships and immigration because it is Fantasy? Can Miéville or Hutchinson make no comment on European politics through alternate history? Are we now to dismiss Hopkinson's vital works on race politics in Canada?

Having spent last week co-running a symposium with the theme 'Escaping Escapism in Fantasy and the Fantastic' (GIFCon 2018), I can safely say Walter's remarks about dangerous escapism are startling out of step with current academic thinking. Le Guin, Miyazaki Hayao, Tolkien, and many fantasy theorists have spoken on the usefulness of fantasy and SF for social commentary and enabling much-needed empathy – less escaping *from*, but *into* a space in which these issues can be confronted directly. Through genre, assumptions underlying the everyday are estranged from their contexts, allowing us to better examine and question their value. Undeniably, this is the aim of Atwood's alternate present. Perhaps Walter can't be blamed for such easy mistakes. In the 1970s, Darko Suvin carved out space for legitimate academic study of SF by emphasizing its differences from fantasy – and setting back fantastic academia by decades. Nearly 50 years later, literary studies have moved on, and so should we. Such dismissive attitudes speak less of genuine concern for genre assignment, more a wish to divorce an author from the varied facets of their works.

There remains one certainty in this debate: once a writer has released a book, for better or worse, she ceases to have full control over its reception. Some writers sacrifice a reliable audience for the potential of a bigger market, hoping to influence that a little. But, whichever genre you choose, there are no guarantees of how your work may be received, or by whom. While SF has had issues with closed-minded elements, attitudes like Walter's risk blaming far right anti-feminist attitudes on innocent writers – and innocent readers. Few genres have escaped association with unsavoury movements. After all, the biggest influence on neoliberalist politics is Ayn Rand, whose works are usually found in bookshops under – that's right – the General Fiction section.

1 David Barnett (2015), 'Kazuo Ishiguro thinks his fantasy novel is not a fantasy novel. Are we bothered?', *The Guardian*, https://www.theguardian.com/books/booksblog/2015/mar/05/kazuo-ishiguro-the-buried-giant-fantasy-novel [accessed 2 May 2018]

2 Pippa Goldschmidt (2018), 'Interview: Helen Sedgwick',*Shoreline of Infinity 10*, pp. 106.

3 'An open letter to The Bookseller', *Gollancz*, https://www.gollancz.co.uk/2018/05/an-open-letter-to-the-bookseller/ [accessed 3 May 2018]

4 Damien E. Walter (2017), 'No, The Handmaid's Tale is not Science Fiction', *Medium*, https://medium.com/@damiengwalter/no-the-handmaids-tale-is-not-science-fiction-d1572a1876de [accessed 2 May 2018]

Ruth EJ Booth is an award-winning writer, editor, and academic based in Glasgow, Scotland. For stories and more, see www.ruthbooth.com.

Seven Surrenders and The Will to Battle (Books 2 and 3 of Terra Ignota)
Ada Palmer
Head of Zeus, 368 & 352 pages
Review by Eris Young

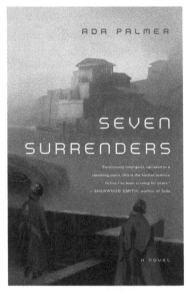

Terra Ignota is the story of a collapsing world. The quadrilogy, books two and three of which were released in the UK late last year, takes place in a seemingly utopian society carefully stewarded by an elite ruling class. The narrative is the story of these stewards, the leaders of each government, or hive, who operate outside the awareness of the average citizen. At the end of the first book, *Too Like the Lightning*, a conspiracy comes to light that threatens to topple the entire structure. In book two, *Seven Surrenders*, the dangers of war for a gentle world full of medical nanotechnology and bioengineered luxuries is fully revealed. After an assassination attempt tips the world closer to danger, Bridger, a young boy with miraculous powers, makes the ultimate sacrifice to give the world a war hero to guide it through the time ahead. Book three follows the world powers through a series of strained negotiations, shepherded by this new hero, and as disaster strikes at the end of the third book, *The Will to Battle*, it seems that war has finally arrived.

Narrated by Mycroft Canner, servant to all seven hives and certified madman, the *Terra Ignota* books take place over just a few frenetic days. The reader is given a highly-detailed view of the world's political microcosm as the delicate equilibrium of the hives is upset (be aware that there will be slight spoilers in this review as I talk about how this equilibrium is upset).

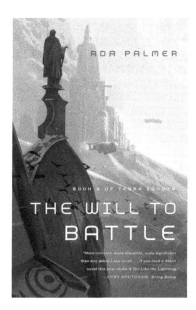

ADA PALMER

BOOK 3 OF TERRA IGNOTA

THE WILL TO
BATTLE

"More intricate, more plausible, more significant
than any debut I can recall... If you read a debut
novel this year, make it *Too Like the Lightning*."
— CORY DOCTOROW, *Boing Boing*

Perhaps one of the most notable aspects of the first book in the series, *Too Like the Lightning* (reviewed in *Shoreline of Infinity* issue 10), is Palmer/Canner's lush, even indulgent description of every setting, character and conversation. This serves a practical purpose: to give the 21st century reader a crash course in 25th century culture. But it also serves a narrative one: in *Seven Surrenders* and *The Will to Battle*, the utopian society that seemed entirely lacking in conflict is revealed to be a fiction, built on a foundation of corruption, murder and quasi-incest.

In a shrewd parallel, Canner's narration is itself called into question, and other characters, whose accounts are included like evidence in a tribunal, repeatedly question his judgment. This reinforces the building sense of unease and dissonance which eventually explodes at the end of *Seven Surrenders*.

It was over the course of this middle volume that the series won me over. Where Palmer obfuscated in the first book, here she explains. I experienced several moments of epiphany in *Seven Surrenders* where details clicked into place, and the full scale of the conspiracy on which the conflict rests began to be revealed.

In book two the wholesome, even saccharine, dialogue and customs depicted in book one are replaced by—or revealed to be a facade masking—perversion, corruption, a rotten core. This payoff is one of Palmer's greatest narrative successes; there were several instances in books two and three that had me gasping aloud despite myself, scandalised.

If *Seven Surrenders* was devoted to revealing some rather jarring complexities in the worldbuilding set up by book one, book three, *The Will to Battle*, is dedicated to documenting how that complexity—those mistakes, those hidden fetishes, that corruption, those lies—are tipping this carefully tended system towards global, devastating war, despite the best efforts of all the king's horses and all the king's men. There is a gathering urgency in *The Will to Battle* that throws the micro-scale of the story into sharp relief, and the second-by-second telling of the final scene in book three, detailing the exact moment war breaks out, suggests book four will be even more gripping.

In a recent Reddit AMA, Palmer was asked why her books seem to focus on the influence of "great men and women" instead of the power of the people. The cascade of events of book three belie this assumption: the great actors whom we've followed from the beginning—and who've been set up as nearly infallible in *Too Like the Lightning*, are swept along on a tide of public outrage, fear and panic.

Just as the best stories are ones that challenge the status quo, I maintain that the best books about powerful people are about their vulnerabilities. The narratives I'm interested in are those that take a system—whether it exists in real life or not—and subverts it. In *Terra Ignota* chroniclers are revealed to be madmen, peace is bought with violence, enlightenment is built on fallacy, and all the rulers of the world are in thrall to a monster of their own making.

More than the fancy language, the worldbuilding and the literary references, these reversals in status, the hamartia and the fall, are what make *Terra Ignota* compelling. And just as the leaders are carried on an inexorable tide towards war, the rising tension and explosive action in books two and three have carried me along, almost against my will. I can't wait for the next book.

The fourth book in the Terra Ignota *series,* Perhaps the Stars, *will be released sometime in 2019.*

A Scruffian Survival Guide
Hal Duncan
Lule, 118 pages
Reviewed by Steve Ironside

Language is a marvel. The formality of words and structure, the ends to which it can be put – poetry, technical description, the odd bawdy chat down the pub; allowing communication in ways both broad and narrow. And yet, it remains very personal, with dialects, accents and colloquialisms meaning that there are as many ways of using it as there are stars in the sky. As Stephen Fry once put it, "There is no right language or wrong language any more than there are right or wrong clothes." Mixing up your own palette of language then, is something that should be applauded and explored – which is what Hal Duncan has done with *A Scruffian Survival Guide*.

The book is an anthology of tales, which draws a picture of a hidden community of children (the "Scruffians" of the title) who have survived in the shadows since the Crusades, having been "Fixed" – that is, had their ageing halted through the use of a mystical Stamp. This process renders them truly immortal – they can be mutilated, killed, starved – it makes no difference as they will spring back the next day in exactly the same state they were in when they were Fixed.

It goes without saying that adults – "groanhuffs" – abuse them terribly as a result. Fixing them at different ages for different purposes, from scamps used as drummer boys, to rakes who are nearly too old (and have too much wilfulness) for use as soldiers. A slave race, with no need to be fed, no repercussions if killed, and as a result thoroughly ground under the heel of their masters. It appears that resistance would be impossible.

Except that it's not. The Scruffians have managed to throw off their oppressors, have stolen back the Stamp that created them, and learned how to get the most out of their state of being. Those lessons are then passed along using an oral tradition with stories – "fabbles" – told by the longest-lived Scruffians to the youngest. A mix of nursery rhymes, fairy tales, and retellings of heroic adventures. *A Scruffian Survival Guide* is (effectively) a transcript of the telling of some of these fabbles to a group of new recruits, clueing them in on what they need to know to get by.

I'd probably have failed that particular test, as for me this was a tough book to crack. Our storyteller (let's call him "Jack" as other unnamed Scruffians are) is a centuries-old lad, with a very thick Coc-ker-nee accent and a chatty style of speaking. He's also not averse to chatting with some of his friends at the same time as telling a story to the assembled scamps, or dealing with their heckling and interruption. Mixing this in with the way that fabbles are told, switching back and forth from tale to rhyme, and the liberal smattering of Scruffian-specific dialect, I found that following the thread of what was going on could

get challenging – this is not, after all, a physical conversation where there are lots of non-verbal cues to help you track the focus of the speaker. Also, unlike (for example) the use of NADSAT in Anthony Burgess's *A Clockwork Orange*, there's no handy glossary of terms at the back of the book to help you refresh yourself with the meaning of bits of the lingo, and I found myself flipping backwards and forwards between reading sessions to reference some terms that hadn't quite cemented themselves in my head. As a result, this wasn't a book I felt that I could dip in and out of – I had to commit to finding space to sit down and read, for fear of losing track of what it was trying to show me.

I also didn't find myself drawn in to the individual stories– because the fabbles are either historical reference or purely allegorical, I didn't really care about the characters in them. I felt like I probably should – some of the uses to which a virtually indestructible child can be put are harrowing when described, but when there's just a name and no depth of character, it's harder to empathise. After all, the point is not to care about Aesop's Tortoise or Hare; the importance is in the lesson that fable teaches. In *A Scruffian Guide to Survival*, it feels like the purpose of a fabble is to learn about the world – a travelogue in first person.

And yet what a place to visit! Scruffians learning how to Tweak their Stamps to unexpected and sometimes comic effect; how one can get Scoured out of existence, and the creation of a new generation of Scruffians. Then there are the battles with Hellions, and the links between major world events and these secretive immortal urchins – you do feel that the stories presented here only scratch the surface of what is going on in the author's mind.

There are other books which are set in the Scruffian universe, and although I haven't read them, I wonder if this in some way acts as a companion volume to them – filling in details about this hidden culture. There are definitely some fantastic ideas behind this setting – the notion that there are Scruffians hiding between the cracks of modern society is very appealing – but the challenges I faced in getting to grips with Duncan's writing means that I probably won't seek out his other books to see just how much broader this canvas grows. However, if you can get into the rhythm of the narrative and the approach to the telling of the stories then I don't doubt that this universe can offer hours of entertainment.

On language, Mr. Fry has also said, "The English language is an arsenal of weapons. If you are going to brandish them without checking to see whether or not they are loaded, you must expect to have them explode in your face from time to time.". I'm sure that Hal Duncan used his arsenal well – on this occasion though, I just wasn't wearing enough armour.

You Should Come with Me Now: Stories of Ghosts
M. John Harrison
Comma, 272 pags
Review: Katy Lennon

This collection is clearly the work of a veteran of the short story; yet Harrison's 15 year break from the format obviously did not dull his aptitude or enthusiasm for it. Published by Comma Press, known genre fans committed to showcasing excellent contemporary short fiction, it reads like a bizarre holiday to our own reality, warped in its truthfulness and deceitful in its absurdism.

The stories are at the same time slaves to the horrors of "super-reality" and impish masters of it; existing within the mold of contemporary British culture while paying no mind to its rules and limitations. At the same time, we inhabit a cynical, vacant reality, and a fantastical alternate universe, where characters are unbound by the rules of traditional fiction and stumble towards the realm of fable or fairy tale. Surreal non-fiction, hypnagogic psychogeography and absurdist ghost stories all clamor for attention while Harrison sweeps through them with effortless ease.

"Animals" lets its creepiness

slowly unfurl, as the protagonists' idyllic rented cottage shows itself to be already occupied. The passive aggressions and then later, murderous intent of the cottage's previous tenants builds up to a tense and violent finale. But throughout the story the reader is shown on all sides the primacy and simplicity of the lives of animals; by the end humans are the ones who seem brutal and unknowable, 'just like animals', as Susan wails during the climax of the cottage's violence.

Harrison's prose is crafted with acute awareness, each sentence stretching and twisting the reader's expectations, forcing them into uncomfortable positions of hilarity, disgust, and self-reflection. Some of the stories take place in the world of Autotelia, (literally 'existing for its own sake') and some in the "real" world, though at times it is difficult to tell the two apart. Harrison sits us down with the particularities (and peculiarities) of British identity. Deftly mixing colonialism, relationship strains and societal pressures into strange short stories of seemingly ordinary people faced with the eldritch terrors of the mundane; who either try desperately not to get swallowed, or throw themselves wildly into its gaping maw.

"The Walls" laughs madly in the face of logic, detailing the tedious and slow escape of a man, D, from imprisonment. He has already made great progress with his two dessert spoons and broken nail scissors, digging for 'decades', before he discovers countless corpses of men just like him, trying to escape. Yet, as with most of Harrison's characters, he remains indifferent to this discovery, even mentioning that they 'died doing what they loved'.

Years go by, he breaks through wall after wall, discovering corpse after corpse. Then, he decides to check on his progress, moving back through the tunnels of dead men, through his cell, out of the unlocked door, through the prison complex, then out the front door and round the building to examine the concrete wall he hopes to break through. The story evokes a kind of unhinged nihilism, paired with an almost childlike belief in systems put in place; whether those systems make sense to the reader is of little consequence.

The stories do not usually fit narrative convention, and any reader looking for a complete and satisfying plot might be left wanting. Some stories are abstractly scattered throughout, disappearing and reappearing in 50-100 word morsels, others feel like the first taste of a sprawling epic fantasy novel. Admittedly, some of the shortest pieces seemed part of an elaborate in-joke, one that Harrison seems to be enjoying with himself, and maybe some of his more devoted readers. The overriding feeling throughout is of being washed around in a warm and sweet-scented ocean; you will have no idea where you're going or where you've been, but you'll enjoy being a part of it.

Harrison's collection is at the same time refreshingly new and achingly nostalgic; making scathing societal commentaries while pointing and laughing like some manic, ancient god. Read for surreal apathy from a master of science-fiction, horror, fantasy, and every incarnation in between, not for completely set out plot points and satisfying endings. These short stories don't care whether you understand them or not.

Spare and Found Parts
Sarah Maria Griffin
Titan, 416 pages
Review: Georgina Merry

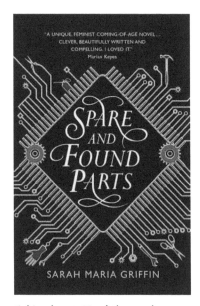

In a post-apocalyptic Ireland where computer technology is banned, Nell Crane, a teen who struggles to fit in, becomes obsessed with building herself a companion. She will stop at nothing to make her fantasy a reality, even if it means rejecting the rules put in place to protect society

Many inhabitants of Black Water Bay were left maimed after The Turn, a deadly epidemic believed to have been caused by advanced technology and artificial intelligence. The plague which ravaged the populace is gone, but electronics and digital tech, referred to as "code", are outlawed for fear of triggering a second outbreak. Clockwork mechanics are embraced, but all tech from before The Turn is considered blasphemous. To ensure everyone's safety, the healed live in The Pasture while the healing, those who are physically blighted, are confined to The Pale; a city we infer was once Dublin. Every citizen is expected to contribute something to society when they come of age and must present their idea in a public forum. Most residents sport artificial limbs or are missing superficial body parts, but not Nell.

Unlike everyone else, Nell's modifications are on the inside. She's marked as different by the scar that runs from her chin to her stomach and her audible, ticking heart. Her father and recently-deceased mother are famous for their scientific skill and contribution to Black Water Bay society. Julian Crane's revolutionary designs for artificial limbs keep them both in high standing, allowing him to conduct mysterious experiments in his laboratory. However, Nell is weighed down by her differences and the looming obligation of providing a contribution of her own. Her greatest fear is that her inventive skill may never live up to her that of her parents. While scavenging for parts, she finds a prosthetic hand which ignites a desire to construct a partner, be they boy or girl, from salvage. Determined to succeed, she uses whatever means possible to achieve her goal, including theft and deception. While she's confident she can build a body, she requires more advanced tech to replicate consciousness. With the assistance of Oliver Kelly, a boy she's loathed since childhood, she meets an underground group of rebels set on bringing back code. Using an old tablet-style phone as a brain, she brings life to Io, an eloquent, observant, intelligent automaton. But her creation is a catalyst, and Nell's life is turned upside down as she uncovers the uncomfortable truth about her parents.

Closer to the sci-fi end of steampunk, as opposed to the Victorian alt-reality characteristic of the genre, *Spare and Found Parts* is set in a far-flung dystopian future. The story is told via an unconventional approach of switching between second and third person narrative perspective. This occurs intermittently, and it's a technique that's difficult to pull off, yet Griffin does so with aplomb. What makes it work well is the way in which the relevance of these narrative shifts is revealed to the reader toward the latter end of the book. Everything comes together neatly in a perfectly designed story that's thoroughly enjoyable. Saying that, not a lot actually happens. As far as most YA is concerned, the plot is fairly inactive. It's the prose that does the heavy lifting. The exquisite, poetic style is poignant and delicate without resorting to superfluous adjectives or flowery imagery. It keeps the momentum moving forward with grace. It's a treat to read something written so beautifully.

Another commendable aspect worth mentioning is how well the author has represented diversity without an agenda. Nell is a bisexual woman of colour, Oliver has same-sex parents, and almost everyone has a physical disability of some sort, be it a missing leg or eye. These have little bearing on the plot, other than the biomechanical inventions, and are never laboured or conveyed through overt means. They're merely part of the characters' identity, as is the way in real life. This simple approach to inclusion is understated but tremendously effective. Here's hoping this is a sign of what we can come to expect from future YA publications.

When it comes to protagonist Nell, the reader is dragged through a gauntlet of emotions ranging from intense irritation to strong admiration. She's flawed, impatient, and difficult to please. There are occasions when it's hard to respect her choices, but equally there are times when it's all too easy to get caught up in her driving passion. Her response to hearing songs from before The Turn is blissful and magnificently conveyed. We hear the music as she does, fresh and unknown, even though we're given clues as to what the songs are. By the end she's confident, strong, and we can't help but be happy for her.

Unlike Nell, Io, the artificial boy, has the ability to comprehend his life and the world around him with compassion. Although, understanding how he comes to have such a distinct personality in such a short space of time requires suspending one's disbelief. Nevertheless, he's charming and humane to the point of highlighting the ignorance of other characters. Then there's Oliver Kelly, who makes no secret of his desire to marry Nell. His dogged pursuit of Nell inspires both revulsion and pity. Yet, as the story unfolds he grows more likeable. The other characters, including Nell's father, are less memorable, but this is a minor grievance with an otherwise splendid cast. If you appreciate gorgeous writing and unpredictable storyline then *Spare and Found Parts* is absolutely worth your time.

Null States
Malka Older
Tor, 432
Review by Callum McSorley

Malka Older returns to the world of *The Centenal Cycle* with her second book in the series, *Null States*. In her debut, *Infomocracy*, she introduced us to a near-future in which 'Information' – a near-ubiquitous, utopian version of the internet where all statements and stories are rigorously fact-checked and attributed through the use of video feeds, polling data and traditional news-gathering techniques—underpins democracy, or rather, micro-democracy.

Here, nation-states such as we are familiar with are gone, the world is divided into centenals of 100,000 people who can move wherever they want to live under whatever government they want, with thousands of would-be governments competing (fairly, thanks to Information) for their votes, including both traditional parties and corporate parties like Philip Morris and 888. It's not as complicated as it sounds, especially if you've read the first book, and is an interesting and fun concept.

Hippy-types move to centenals where weed is legal, smokers to centenals where there is no smoking ban, Americans to centenals where there is no health or social care and the head governor is only really concerned with letting people

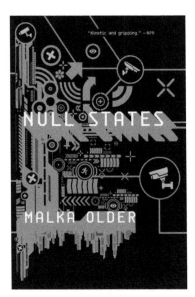

know he has a huge penis… Joking, that would of course be flagged up for investigation and verification by Information—the independent bureau that regulates the system and shares its name.

Protagonist Roz is part of this bureau, and at the beginning of the novel is sent to DarFur, which is new to micro-democracy and needs a helping hand to adjust. When its governor is assassinated, she has to investigate, but given its fledgling status, there is very little Information infrastructure in place and Roz has to go old school to get results, including becoming romantically entangled with a prime suspect—way old school.

This drama is played out over the backdrop of war in the 'null states' – old, reduced nations that refuse to convert to micro-democracy, are mostly isolationist, and therefore aren't part of Information's network. Older's decades of experience in humanitarian aid and development are on full show here, bringing a powerful sense of realism to her sci-fi world.

Main character of *Infomocracy*, Mishima, is on the back-bench until halfway through the novel, which is a shame because she was the most interesting character in the first book, and in this one too. She's a spy and a ninja with a mental illness called 'narrative disorder' which lets her see patterns of intrigue in recalcitrant data that may or may not be there, and she sometimes describes her emotions in colours and shapes. The rest of the diverse cast isn't so well fleshed out, and *Infomocracy's* dull leading man Ken (appropriate name choice) is, thankfully, largely abandoned.

When Mishima is brought in to investigate a large government's threat of secession from micro-democracy, the pace picks up and with it the tension. The expected plot twists, however, fail to come through, with some last-minute reveals falling flat, and some being logically questionable.

Difficult situations always seem to get resolved in some banal way or through a chance event, which is realistic but not satisfying. It also leaves the reader with the feeling that the stakes are not particularly high, therefore it seems ludicrous that while working undercover in a government office, Mishima is always ready with a sharp knife hidden under her clothes— is she really going to murder someone for finding out she is an undercover Information operative? She doesn't seem the type.

Also, it begs the question why Information, whose whole point in being is transparency, has undercover operatives at all. In fact, one of the glaring holes in the story is the lack of criticism aimed at Information. All the main characters in some way belong to Information, and they're the good guys, even if they are undertaking covert and undemocratic missions in order to protect micro-democracy. When they do occasionally question the morality of this they always conclude that what they do is for the greater good.

Even among Information's detractors, nobody is really, truly furious that they've essentially turned the world into one giant surveillance state. There are cameras everywhere, yet nobody uses the terms 'Orwellian' or 'Big Brother'.

This is either a clever comment on our society's current obsession with broadcasting our every move via social media—in this future people are so inured to it that they can't conceive of constant surveillance being a threat in any way—or a wilful oversight. Maybe it will be addressed in the next book.

Null States suffers from the same problem as it predecessor, its mix of action thriller and political drama often doesn't mesh. That said, it has the same strengths too. Mishima is great, the exotic locations are a joy to be in, and micro-democracy and Information are both fascinating ideas that Older has plenty of fun with, and which the reader will be left thinking deeply about long after the (abrupt) end of the novel. Despite my criticisms, I look forward to the next part of the series, slated for publication this year.

Binary System
Eric Brown
Solaris, 400 pages
Review by Lucy Powell

BINARY SYSTEM

'This is the rediscovery of wonder.'
Stephen Baxter on Helix

ERIC BROWN

An amalgamation of two short novellas, *Binary* and *System*, Eric Brown's *Binary System* is a novel that quite literally starts with a bang. After the spaceship Andromeda catastrophically explodes going through a routine wormhole jump, the accident is enough to fling the book's protagonist Cordelia Kemp, sat in her escape pod, tens of thousands of light years through space and time. The problem? Humanity thus far in this novel has only travelled a measly two-hundred. She is, for all intents and purposes, stranded. It is with this horrific yet beautifully realised crushing sense of realisation that Brown leads us into the novel. We accompany Kemp crash landing on a nearby planet (later named 'Valinda') after her life raft is shot down. This alien planet is where the rest of the novel takes place. She battles her way through hostile alien life, establishes First Contact, all the while trying to understand the mysteries of this new planet, survive, and accept the crushing reality that she might never be going home.

In part, the book is a neat addition to the sci-fi genre, and the concept of 'lone survivor on an alien world' is one that Brown explores well. The weird, wonderful, and often deadly creatures Kemp comes across make for a thrill ride as she is captured, escapes and is then hunted across the landscape, finding herself embroiled in a burgeoning civil war between the oppressed race (the Fahran) and their oppressors (the Skelt). The world building however is one that, whilst adhering to well-worn and dependable sci-fi tropes, could have done with more historical context. A twenty-third century pilot drawing upon twenty-first century pop culture references is too anachronistic to stomach.

Whilst the Imp (Kemp's in-built computer implant, without whom her experience on this planet would have assuredly been very different) translates the strange languages, tests the water and air supply, and muddles its way through the stranger parts of what the planet has to offer, one is still left feeling as though there is not enough strangeness present. The alien planet is one which shares very human-like amenities and cultural experiences; ranging from beds, to money and trade routes, to the concept of organised religion (although without giving too much away this 'religion' has a later intriguing, if familiar conclusion).

The main 'twist' of the novel is by and large one you can spot a mile off, although as this is a book that doesn't pride itself on being a mystery novel, that is perhaps not the point. Whilst the writing in some places is jarring, we are seeing this brand new world for the first time much as Kemp is experiencing it. If there are some sentences or concepts that don't quite make sense, it is because she too is struggling to put the world and aliens she encounters into words. The descriptions Brown presents to us of strange worms that rise out of the ground to eat seed pods, in a similar vein to Frank Herbert's *Dune*, and scenes where Kemp introduces the Fahran to the music of Arvö Part are almost ridiculous—but that is perhaps the beauty of it.

Brown's *Binary System* is a colourful romp, and whilst the storyline is not particularly deep or taxing on the imagination, if you like exploratory space-faring science fiction then this is definitely a book to explore.

From Issue 13 we welcome our new Reviews Editor Samantha Dolan. In her own words:

"I've been writing since I could hold a pen and have worked my way from Fantasy to YA to Shakespearean Vampires before arriving almost by accident at sci fi. It's where I live now, where I find, understand and exercise my issues. And they are not few. Beware, dear Readers, this way madness lies."

We have been warned...

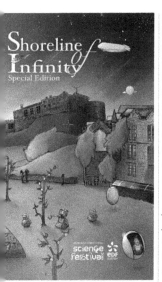

Eye, Tongue, Machinus

So this is home, then; singled off and sectioned
in a cabled cage, my hair reduced to threads
and my skin turning in, form-folded on withering hinges.
I see my life's philosophy easeled on my parts;
there's my conduction rate, and that's an actuator's sparks –
sharp and blue beneath fluorescent lamplight.

Voices enquired if it hurt when they cut out my tongue
but none guessed the answer,
instead they packed my mouth with dirt
and foam, then in quiet tones 'waste not want not' –
the ethical friend of endeavour, but enemy to a tidy end.
You see – that tongue was mine, plaited down my throat
and roped around my larynx, feeding eyes
they infinitely ignore with how to look.
They couldn't have taken more of me.

They care about my falling hair though;
streaks of iridescent copper moving between fingers like
magnetics. Silver men number each follicle
and press in a pin. This care is fractured.
I'd lain for days before my dress was dissolved by the acid bath,
the emergent me all freshly red.
They could have just asked but instead converged
over fussy bits like fingernails, my nose, the rivers of blue
wrist tattoos, giving my skin a score.

I'm feeling lighter all the time. It's not been long
but maybe it's just the excess of arrows on boxes
always pointing down, like mad sprigs determined to grow.
It's wrong, they should face up towards the light,
but I don't know what's right for a room stacked
with cardboard coffins and broken limbs.

And now
though they didn't like their brownness before
they've marked out my eyes for another head;
plucking them from my skull without seeing me within.
Perhaps I'll see again from a different height,
though my peripherals travel so weary and slow,
each thought collapsing into millennia and inactive
on the air like a hoverfly, something still, but alive,
or a glass singing, close to its shatter and stop

Taxes

After she checked herself in,
found her cubicle, stripped
from gaunt thins into surgical linens
and awaited the anaesthetist on duty –
she thought back to her grandmother.

The roundedness of her, an entire earth;
scarred pink from numerous Benidorm afternoons
and boastful flesh; full of herself,
pruned into a cognisant topiary.
Never owing anything to the state, she'd give you
the back of her hand rather than a share of liver,
an eye, or her eustachian tube;
and it would still mean something different to you.

Her body failed her in the end, naturally,
occupied by fostered carcinogens from her little choices.
Her world demanded no court-orders,
carving up the cadaver-in-arrears,
or an official apology for her lifestyle.

Caroline Hardaker

Caroline Hardaker lives and scribbles in Newcastle upon Tyne. Her poetry
has been published widely, most recently by Magma, The Emma Press, The
Interpreter's House, and Eyewear's Best of New British and Irish Poets 2018. Her
debut chapbook 'Bone Ovation' was published by Valley Press in October 2017.

NEW PLANET LANDSCAPE 29

Clinging to the peaks of the calm
virtual mountains, they could breathe
the thinner air, vice languishing down here
where the syrupy atmosphere might inhale
them. But do not think them spindly.
We marvel that these sinewy few climbed
to the top of the land, spread out
to gather the alms of the sun
and shake their spine leaves
at us like warriors' warnings.
There is something commendable in it.
They move glacially, peak to peak,
as we move system to system.
Sunlight in, merciless infestation out.
Only the air keeps them contained.

Ken Poyner

Ken Poyner's collections of brief fictions, *Constant Animals* and *Avenging Cartography*, as well as poetry *The Book of Robot* and *Victims of a Failed Civics*, can be located through links at www.barkingmoosepress.com. He has had recent work out in *Analog, Asimov's, Café Irreal*, and other places, both print and web.

Elizabeth Dulemba is an author, illustrator, teacher, and speaker (TED). Her newest title is 'Crow not Crow' by Jane Yolen and Adam Stemple. She holds an MFA from the University of Edinburgh, is a PhD Researcher at the University of Glasgow, and is Visiting Associate Professor at Hollins University.
www.dulemba.com

Forest

End of the hallway,
Portal to worlds beyond,
Journey to elsewhere.

Stag Beetle Princess

Do not let my size
lull a false sense of safety.
We are warriors all.

Mechanical Beast

Snap, crank, stomp whir, squee.
I traverse the desert with
solar panelled ears.

Elizabeth Dulemba

Just for Fun - Spot the Difference

Being doodles loosely* based on a SF classic,
Can you spot 10 differences between these two images by TSU BEEL?

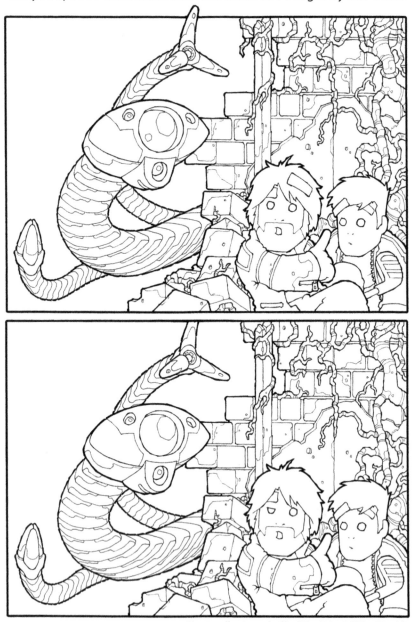

*ie, totally ripped off of The War Of The Worlds